BORN CHOSEN

To order additional copies of

Born Chosen,

by

Mark Witas,

call

1-800-765-6955.

Visit us at

www.reviewandherald.com

for information on other Review and Herald® products.

BORN CHOSEN

An adopted son,

a mother's search,

and God's perfect providence

MARK WITAS

REVIEW AND HERALD® PUBLISHING ASSOCIATION
HAGERSTOWN, MD 21740

The author assumes full responsibility for the accuracy of all facts and quotations as cited in this book.

This book was
Edited by Penny Estes Wheeler
Copyedited by Delma Miller and James Cavil
Cover designed by Square One Design
Interior designed by Trent Truman
Electronic makeup by Shirley M. Bolivar
Typeset: 12/15 Bembo

PRINTED IN U.S.A.

06 05 04 03 02 5 4 3 2 1

R&H Cataloging Service
Witas, Mark, 1962-
Born chosen

1. Witas, Mark, 1962- 2. Spiritual life. I. Title.

B

ISBN 0-8280-1687-9

THANKS

I owe the inspiration and desire

to write this book

to my family—new and old;

to my wife and son;

and especially to my mother—both of you.

CONTENTS

PREFACE

I'd never been one to question why things happened; I just figured that they did. Once in a while I'd look at an experience and wonder if God's hand had broken into my existence and saved me or directed things. But for the most part I assumed life just happened.

I had my reasons for drawing this conclusion. First, I'd noticed life happens pretty randomly. I remember thinking that it would be so neat and tidy if bad people were stricken with terminal diseases and good people always enjoyed health and success, but early on I discovered this is not the case. Both good, moral people and those with questionable lifestyles—the politically correct term for "bad people"—enjoy success and battle pain. It's true that many who smoke get lung cancer; but some don't, and live till they're 98. Some people who stay with strict, healthy diets live till they're 102. But others with the same diet get cancer or heart disease and die at an early age.

As I said, life just happens. Right?

I believe God created us with a free will. That's another reason I've always assumed life just happens. At the risk of sounding deistic, to me "free will" meant that life happened without God twisting my arm or forcing me to do or become anything. He was free to use whatever means He needed in order to get my attention, but that's where His involvement stopped. I always assumed that having free will meant that my life could take any direction I wanted it to without any interference from God.

And finally, my idea that life just happens came from the fact that

I am phlegmatic both in personality and in my outlook on life. I've never been driven by guilt or embarrassment to become or do anything. I've never seen God as someone who would drive me this way or that because of my behavior, good or bad. I always figured He would save His involvement with me for judgment day—whenever that was. Other than that, my life was what *I* made it.

Being phlegmatic meant that I never concerned myself with the future. I'm not sure that I've ever actually applied for a job (this really frustrates my friends). Why worry about it? Life just happens, right? On a spiritual note, I'd never been concerned about "when" Christ would return. I always figured that if I were living right today, tomorrow would take care of itself.

To a large extent, this philosophy guided most of my early life. And then one quiet Friday evening I received a phone call that permanently changed my thinking.

You see, in a moment's time my "uninvolved" God got my attention and gave me a new paradigm, a new idea about who He is and how involved He'd been in my life all along. That's what this book is about. I will also share some lessons I've learned since then, lessons that I believe make up the crux of the gospel.

DISCLAIMER

As I tell you my story, realize that I am still piecing it together. It's possible that some of what you are about to read may have happened a little differently than I remember. Unfortunately, some of the key players are no longer available to help with the puzzle. Also, a few names have been changed to protect anonymity. This is my life—told through the view of those who have lived it with me, and as I remember it. I hope it will give you hope and a new concept of how deeply God is involved in *your* life, and has been all along.

CHAPTER 1

LIFE HAPPENS

The Baby Store

My dad's version of my origins in our family goes something like this.

After about 10 years of marriage my parents figured out that they weren't going to have kids the "old-fashioned way," so they decided to try a different method. My dad tells me that he and Mom decided to go to the baby store and buy themselves a baby. Sounds suspicious, doesn't it? Well, that's his story and he's sticking to it.

So, he says, he and Mom went to the baby store and discovered that the babies were sorted by size. My parents started looking in the extra-small section of the baby store. They saw some nice babies there, but they felt as though they needed one with more substance. As they moved through the medium-sized babies to the large-sized babies they noticed down in the extra-large section a baby that seemed to need a home more than the others. It was me! "This is the one we want," they said. They wrote a check out for about $3,000 and brought me home.

I know about how much money my dad had to shell out because later on in life when I'd fuss about having to mow the lawn, he'd pull out the receipt and say, "We paid good money for you. Now go mow the lawn!" Who could argue with that? Dad still has a great sense of humor.

In all actuality my parents had decided to adopt a baby and found me as a ward of the state in a foster home when I was just a few weeks old.

The first challenge they faced was what to name me. My mom wanted to name me David Timothy. My dad wanted Oscar David. They settled on Mark Andrew. I feel eternal gratitude to my mother for preventing years of my having to endure cruel classmates singing the Oscar Meyer wiener song to me.

Two years into our sojourn together, my parents decided that I needed a sibling. They went back to the baby store and found a little sister for me. Now, I'm not sure, but I think they paid less for her than they did for me. I do know that I had to do more chores around the house than she did. I figured you get what you pay for.

From the beginning, my sister and I knew that we were adopted. My mom would say, "All the other moms just had to take what they got, but your dad and I chose you because we wanted you more than all the other babies at the baby store."

This made me feel pretty special. Being chosen over all the other babies they *could* have purchased at the baby store gave me an early sense of security and specialness. As far as I could tell, the kids who looked like their moms and dads didn't have that advantage. I never had any problems with being adopted.

Being chosen by adoption gave me the certainty that there is no such thing as an illegitimate child, just illegitimate parents. I was blessed to be chosen by parents who loved me and cared for my needs. I will always thank God for that.

To Church or Not to Church—That's the Question

It was about the time that Mom started thinking of having children that she began questioning the kind of life she wanted her future kidlets to have. As she thought this through she realized that she was lacking any kind of spiritual life. She began pondering whether she ought to think about church attendance, and if so, which church she should choose. Two experiences directed her path to join the Seventh-day Adventist Church.

First, my mother's grandmother was a Seventh-day Adventist. Mom's father died while she was just a young girl, and during the time of adjustment after his death Mom stayed with her gramma Sath for several months. During Mom's stay there, Gramma Sath took her to church every Saturday. This limited exposure to the Adventist Church was a seed that grew to bear fruit much later in Mom's life. Gramma Sath's influence on Mom and her siblings was more powerful and lasting than anyone could have ever known.

Many years had passed before the day that Mom was sorting through the mail and found a pamphlet that caught her interest. On its front cover she saw a picture of a loosely dressed wild-eyed woman, a dragon, and current world leaders. In the background hovered a nuclear cloud. On one side was a frowning dark-eyed man with the numerals 666 tattooed on his forehead. In another corner a small group of people knelt in prayer, a ray of light shining upon them. Mom opened the pamphlet and saw that it advertised meetings that were to be held shortly. The meetings seemed religious, but she couldn't find anything that identified the church group that was sponsoring them.

She showed my dad the pamphlet and asked him what he thought. He looked at it for a second and said, "What kind of nut case is putting this stuff out?"

Mom took the pamphlet and put it in her purse.

The next day at work Mom sat down to eat lunch with a good friend of hers. As they talked, Mom pulled the pamphlet from her purse. To her surprise, her friend said, "Hey! That's my church. We're the ones sponsoring the meetings. You ought to come. I'll meet you there."

Mom came home and told my dad that she was going to the meetings. He didn't particularly like the idea, but she went anyway.

It was toward the end of the evangelistic series that Mom decided to be baptized and join the Seventh-day Adventist Church. As Dad tells the story, "I came home from work one night, and your mother was standing in the living room. She was wearing no makeup, no jewelry, and had on this really ugly, plain-looking granny dress." (Mom was never one to do something halfway.)

Dad was confused. "What's going on?" he asked.

Mom's tone was somber. "I'm going to be a Seventh-day Adventist now."

Dad actually tried to do church for about seven years. He was even a deacon for a little while. But he could never quit smoking, and the whole church experience just never took. He wasn't able to experience the same faith that Mom was so excited about. He just wanted to live a normal life like everybody else, while Mom wanted to be a Seventh-day Adventist. Adding children to the mix just complicated the picture. The battle was set.

Sprouts, Meatballs, and Sabbath School

My family was never big on tradition. In fact, the only family tradition that we ever followed was on Sunday afternoons. Just about every Sunday afternoon we'd all sit down in front of the TV and watch black-and-white Tarzan movies, eat Kentucky Fried Chicken, then watch *Star Trek*. Not a particularly meaningful tradition, but our tradition nonetheless.

One memorable Sunday Mom came home from work with a couple of bags of groceries instead of a bucket of fried chicken. She announced to Dad, my sister, and me that we were going to become vegetarians. Now, Dad grew up in Manhattan in a Polish Catholic family. Meat was served at every meal. A meal without meat was incomplete. My dad asked, "Veggie whats?"

"Vegetarians. We are doing it for our health."

That was a half-truth. Somebody at the church had convinced Mom that if she wanted to be a true Seventh-day Adventist she needed to give up flesh foods. Mom was convinced that if she could get my sister and me off flesh foods we would be more translatable (more apt to make it to heaven when Jesus returned). Someone at church had told her that Ellen White, one of the church's founders, said that meat eaters wouldn't make the final cut before Christ comes.

I well remember our vegetarian phase. In the beginning, Mom didn't know a lot about fake meat products or vegetarian casseroles. She set the table with raw fruits, nuts, and grains. We didn't even get anything to drink (something else she picked up from a right-wing militant vegetarian pamphlet). But we were game. We started to eat. We chewed. We tore. We chewed some more. That first foray into vegetarianism must have taken 90 minutes to eat. I thought I'd be a candidate for dentures by the third grade. All that grinding had to have taken a toll on my teeth.

At the end of the meal Dad looked at Mom and said, "OK, nice picnic. Tomorrow I want meatballs. Big ones. Red in the middle." I was hoping that he'd plead my case too, but he didn't. Mom decided to cook meat for him, but to raise my sister and me as grass-eating rabbits. This gave my dad and me many occasions to pass the cooked dead stuff under the table while Mom was in the kitchen getting me more browned tofu.

Mom never did anything halfway, and another of her phases was "supper for breakfast." Normally we'd wake up to Cream of Wheat, or waffles, or my personal favorite, Lucky Charms. During Mom's new phase we'd wake up to veja links, broccoli, and a baked potato. That phase lasted until Mom figured out how much easier it was to pour a bowl of cereal in the morning than to cook a four-course meal.

Another source of my early religious confusion was Saturdays. At some point Mom and Dad sort of agreed to share us on Saturdays, and on the Saturdays Mom was in charge of me we went to Sabbath school and church. To my chagrin, this meant that we couldn't watch cartoons. I had to get up early, take a shower, get my hair combed—you know, all the stuff little boys hate—then rush off to church.

Now, Sabbath school was a blast. We got to wave flags, play with felts, do the Father Abraham dance, and bang sticks together. I loved Sabbath school. Church, however, was a different story.

Church, to a 5-year-old, is cruel and unusual restraint. It's tapping your mom on the shoulder 15 times during the sermon and asking, "Is he almost done?" It's having to go to the bathroom every five minutes and needing a drink every three. It's sitting quietly with a bag of Cherrios on your lap while the pastor pontificates on this week's continuing series on the soteriological and eschatological implications of the book of Numbers. I loved Sabbath school and loathed church.

After church it got more complicated. Saturday had its own set of rules. Sometimes Mom would take us with some of her friends from church to the beach. On hot sunny days we could wade, but not swim. ("They baptize people on Sabbath," I told my mom. "Why can't we get our heads wet?") At home we couldn't ride our bikes, but we could go on grueling hikes in "God's nature." I remember sitting with the church bulletin—the hour and minute that the sun went down was always printed on the inside page—and watching the clock on our mantel, waiting for the minute we could turn on the TV or go out and play with our friends.

(I wonder if Adam and Eve had church bulletins with sundown times printed in them. I think that if we're always checking the church bulletin to see when Sabbath is going to be over, Sabbath isn't doing us much good in the first place. I wish churches would stop printing the time that the sun goes down. I'm pretty sure all it's used for is to help people plan what they're going to do when Sabbath is over.)

On the Saturdays that my dad had me, we went places and did things that I liked to do. Occasionally he'd take me to see the Washington Huskies play football. I loved college football. I'd be sitting next to him clutching a Coke and my stadium hot dog—covered with hot mustard and onions. Every once in a while he'd lean over and look at me with a suspicious grin on his face. "Whatcha got there?"

"A hot dog." He should know. He bought it for me.

"What's in the hot dog?" he'd ask.

"I dunno."

"Oink, oink," he'd say. (I knew Mom's thoughts on eating meat, especially pig meat, and I knew what he was doing.)

"What are you drinking?"

"A Coke."

"What's in the Coke?"

"What?" I'd ask.

"Caffeine." (I knew Mom's thoughts on caffeine-tainted beverages.)

"What day is it?" he'd continue.

"Saturday?"

"It's the *Sabbath.*" Then he'd lean over, look at me, and say, "God'll getcha."

I expected a huge thumb to come out of the sky and squish me right there in the stadium for being a pork-eating, caffeine-drinking Sabbathbreaker.

As a kid, it was hard for me to get any kind of spiritual balance. A child tries to learn the difference between right and wrong. When parents give mixed signals on what is spiritually right and wrong, often kids are forced to choose between what's fun and not fun instead of realizing the spiritual implications. It was at a fairly young age that I decided Dad was more fun than Mom. Football games were more fun than church. Fishing was more fun than church. Anything was more fun than church.

My sister and I were being polarized by parents who had adopted different moral and spiritual values. And they argued about it almost every night. It's no wonder that Seventh-day Adventism—and other religious groups—strongly discourage people from marrying outside of their faith. It can be hell for the married couple, and worse for the kids.

That's What Friends Are For

Both my parents worked for a living. This meant that until we were about 12, my sister and I had sitters. Our sitters lived a few houses down the street from us. They were nice people, as sitters go, but they didn't have a clue as to what my sister and I were up to most of the day. As long as we showed up every couple of hours and shouted "We're still not dead!" they seemed to be satisfied. This kind of summer and after-school life provided me with a lot of freedom, freedom that a kid that age shouldn't enjoy.

My neighborhood was packed with kids my age. Growing up in that kind of atmosphere is OK if you are a little angel, but I'm afraid my friends and I were angels of another kind. A group of kids roaming around with nearly unlimited unsupervised freedom is tantamount to a group of monkeys left to fend for themselves in a china shop. We were into everything. It's so easy for even conscientious kids to go along with group pressure and do things they wouldn't normally do on their own. Our group wasn't any different. Most of the time we were off playing football or basketball in someone's yard. But there were those *other* times.

We had a tree house in my neighbor's yard, right behind my house, where many of us would sleep during the summer months. We'd squeeze into our club house like sardines and fall asleep telling scary stories and dirty jokes (most of which we didn't understand). When we were preadolescent, the tree house became our place for practical jokes, group experimentation, and discovery.

Our practical jokes were pretty harmless. We'd sneak into the local cemetery and pour liquid soap into all of the fountains, sneak into our friends' parents' houses in the middle of the night and rearrange their furniture, or let the air out of our grumpy neighbor's tires. One night we outdid ourselves and pulled up some of the carrots in my neighbor's backyard garden and replaced them with plastic ones. Maybe there's a reason I'm a youth pastor after all.

If my friends and I had stuck to this kind of mischief, maybe I would have been taken down a different road. Unfortunately, we didn't always stop at harmless fun.

One evening, the summer before I began fifth grade, my friends and I were in the tree house when Kenny said, "Hey, guys, if I show you something, do you promise not to tell?"

Now, Kenny was 2 years older than the rest of us and something of a leader, so we should have been suspicious. But six flashlights suddenly lit up Kenny's face, accompanied by promises that we would keep his secret. Kenny reached into his front pocket and slowly pulled out a package of Marlboro cigarettes. He put one in his mouth and asked, "You guys smoke?"

He knew good and well that we didn't smoke. But knowing that Kenny did smoke, we all vigorously nodded our heads, saying, "Yeah, we smoke, Kenny; yeah, we smoke."

To our collective and individual horror, Kenny started pulling cigarettes out of the pack and poking them in our now-gaping mouths. "Then you won't mind smoking with me," he said smugly.

Some of the cigarettes were placed filter in, some filter out. It was dark. Kenny went from one boy to the next, lighting the cigarettes and instructing each of his pupils how to inhale and exhale properly. One by one my friends inhaled the toxic smoke, coughed, sputtered, wheezed, and shed tears of pain while choking out the words "This is great!" Inevitably each boy doubled over with violent coughing spasms. Kenny and the rest of the gang laughed and chastised them for their distress.

As Kenny's lighter neared my face I developed a plan that I hoped would save me the embarrassment and pain my friends had suffered. One of the few real talents that I'd developed by age 10 was the ability to swallow huge amounts of oxygen and belch out the alphabet, the national anthem, and any other requests my friends might have. My plan was to use this talent as a savior from pain and humiliation.

Kenny lit my cigarette. I drew in a big mouthful of smoke, swallowed it into my stomach, and then faked an inhale. Beams from everyone's flashlight shone on my face. "Now exhale," Kenny commanded.

I exhaled. No smoke came out.

Kenny's eyes got big. "Where'd the smoke go?"

It was a good question. Where was the smoke? I began to panic. Somewhere, lingering in my body, was a bunch of toxic, nasty cigarette smoke. My face must have revealed my panic, and my friends began to laugh. It wasn't funny to me. Desperately I was trying for all I was worth to get the smoke out of my stomach—or wherever it was. Finally I felt it building, and then it happened. I delivered a thunderous belch—one only a fourth grader could truly appreciate—and with it, smoke. The smoke didn't shoot from my mouth and nose, it just kind of floated out. With the flashlights shining on my face, it had a kind of halo effect. It was the most severe humiliation I'd experienced in my short 10 years.

That's kind of how things worked in my neighborhood. One of the guys would be daring enough to introduce something new, and we'd all give it a shot. It wasn't long before there wasn't much we wouldn't try. Some of us could try something new and leave it at that. But it seemed that others of our group had a natural bent for drug and alcohol abuse and took the stuff to extremes. Little did we kids know as we went rollicking from one stupid thing to another that eventually alcohol and drugs would ruin some of our marriages, land some of us in jail, and actually kill one of our close-knit group.

What did we know? We were just kids with nobody around to tell us any different.

Back to the Not-So-"OK" Corral

I loved my family. And I have to say that Dad and Mom tried hard to make our family a successful one. Growing up, we did all kinds of things together as a family that created lasting memories that I'll always treasure.

Each summer we set aside a weekend or two to drive to eastern Washington to Fish Lake, one of our favorite camping spots. Dad and I would hike through the swamp, stand on the big logjam that reached out into the lake (it was really a slow-flowing river), and catch a basketful of rainbow and eastern brook trout. Mom would cook them up, and we'd have a feast.

Dad also took me on an annual "bumming-around" trip. Bumming around was Dad's name for loading up the car with sleeping bags and salami sandwiches, getting in, turning the ignition key, and driving . . . somewhere. We never had a plan, but we had wonderful adventures together.

Once we ended up on the very tip of Washington State looking across the straits to Canada. On our way back down the trail to the car, I pulled out a watchcase that I'd found in the back seat and started opening and closing it. Suddenly Dad picked up a stick and told me to stand off the trail behind the tree while he went on ahead. I couldn't figure out what he was doing. Finally it dawned on me that he'd heard the noise I was making with the watchcase and thought it was someone trying to break into our car. We laughed about that one all the way back home.

We had a good family, and we were happy for the most part. But in spite of our happiness, with each new year came increased marital and spiritual polarity. Mom and Dad kept drawing apart.

Even though I was a child, I knew the source of my parents' marital stress. Mom wanted to raise my sister and me as happy little Seventh-day Adventists. Dad wanted to raise us as happy little pagans. Don't get me wrong. He didn't want to raise us to be morally reprehensible; he just wanted to raise us like he was raised—decent, unchurched kids. Mom wanted us to be trained into a lifestyle that was by my dad's standards (and by the world's standards) odd. Mom took the biblical injunction of 1 Peter 2:9 seriously. She wanted us to be truly "peculiar people."

That made my dad, and at times my sister and me, pretty uncomfortable.

Things really blew up when my mom started pushing the idea of our going to an Adventist school. For the life of him, Dad couldn't figure out why anyone would pay a good amount of money every month for a private education when the school just down the road was free. Mom was already paying tithe—taking 10 percent of their income and putting it in an offering plate. Now she wanted to spend more money on the church. Church school became the topic of regular and heated discussions.

Mom won that battle. I started my fourth-grade year in a private Adventist school. I liked the school and made friends fast. I recognized a lot of the kids from church. It wasn't long before I felt comfortable with the school and my new friends. Dad never got used to the idea, though.

I was in the sixth grade when my parents' marriage suffered what seemed to be the inevitable. Parental arguing was something that I had listened to all my life. Some people sleep to the noise of a fan in their room. Some people are soothed by the sound of a ticking clock. My sister and I learned to sleep peacefully through yelling and screaming.

Usually the arguing would reach a fever pitch, ending in slammed doors and silence. But one night it ended differently. Mom and Dad were arguing about private school again. The argument escalated to the point where Dad blew a fuse. He started using colorful metaphors in creative ways—like the proverbial sailor—and Mom followed suit with cleaner language at ear-shattering tones. I still remember how it ended. Dad just stopped and said, "That's it. I can't do this anymore."

I remember hearing him walk down the hall to the closet next to my room where we kept our suitcases. I heard the closet door open, then close. My parents' room was across from mine. I heard the suitcases snap open, drawers being emptied, and my mom begging my dad to change his mind. My ears followed their footsteps down the hall to the living room.

Mom must have felt desperate. Her last words were "Bob, if Jesus were to knock on this door right now and you were to open it, and He was standing there saying, 'Bob, follow Me,' what would you do?"

"I'd be a fool not to follow Him, if it was actually Him and I knew it."

"Don't you see that He's knocking on your door right now? Can't you see that?"

"I *can't* see that. I don't get how you see it. I've gotta go."

Dad left.

It was a few days later that Mom and Dad sat my sister and me down to break the news to us. We'd heard the argument, so we knew what was coming. Still, my sister cried deep tears. I'm convinced to this day that some of her life choices were a reaction to the divorce and how it shattered her spirit. For years afterward she prayed every night that Mom and Dad would hook back up. But they didn't.

I tried to act tough. I looked at them and said, "Good. I'm sick of you guys fighting all the time."

"You heard us arguing?" they asked, seemingly surprised. "When?"

They tried to assure my sister and me that the divorce had nothing to do with us. We knew differently. We knew the stress that our new school and religion had placed on their marriage. But in reality there wasn't a way to place blame on anyone. Mom and Dad were traveling down different roads, and weren't interested in traveling together anymore.

Though Dad moved a few miles away, he stayed in our lives. We got to see him anytime we wanted. He started dressing differently, driving a Firebird, and dating. That was strange. The girls he brought home were young and pretty. It's scary when you're old enough to be attracted to the girls your dad dates. Of course, it didn't seem like they were much older than I was.

Mom cried for months. She was heartbroken. She was also—suddenly—a single parent, and determined to raise us to the best of her ability.

Happy, Happy Halfway House

I actually loved our new life. I had so much more fun with Dad at his new place than I ever did at home. I often spent weekends with him, and we'd do all the fun things that we never seemed to get around to when he lived at home. I know that divorce was supposed to scar me and give me deep, unresolved inner dilemma, but I kind of liked the attention.

For a kid like me who wanted freedom, life with a single mom was better than I'd had before. I'd already had a lot of freedom when Dad lived at home. Now that he was gone, I had only Mom to deal with. By the time I was in fifth grade I was bigger than my mom, and she was at a loss on how to discipline me. Also, her life was filled with her workplace and the church. I was busy with school and my neighborhood chums. My sister and I would do our chores—all the while watching TV and eating junk food—then go out and play with our friends. It was a pretty uncomplicated life.

Mom must have needed a life of her own, too, because now and then she'd leave us for weekends to go visit her brother and sister-in-law in Walla Walla, Washington, a five-hour drive away. She'd leave Friday after work and come back on Sunday afternoon. Sometimes we stayed with Dad, but often we were alone two nights and days, more or less taking care of ourselves.

During the spring of my eighth-grade year, Mom started spending every single weekend at our uncle's house in Walla Walla. We didn't mind. We were either with Dad or at home with all our friends over. Then one Sunday afternoon Mom came home with a bright look in her eyes and an announcement. She sat us down and dropped the bombshell.

"I'm getting married."

"Mom, you're not even dating anybody!" I gasped. To me, the logic was clear. She couldn't be getting married. No way.

"But I *have* been seeing someone," Mom informed us. "I met him in Walla Walla."

"Who is he, Mom?" we asked. "Do Aunt Maygene and Uncle Mickey know him?"

"Yes, they know him."

"Where did you meet him?"

Then she spilled the beans. "Well, kids, that's the thing. I met him at the state penitentiary, at a prison picnic."

"Mom!" We were horrified. "Tell us he's a guard or something!"

"No, kids; he's not," she said cheerfully. "He's an inmate at the Walla Walla State Penitentiary." The smile never faded from her face.

"How long has he been there?" I shrieked.

Still smiling. "About 18 years."

We sat there in silence. In shock. Then one of us asked the dreaded question: "Mom, what did he do?"

Her smile faded just a little. "Kids, I think he's in for murder. He was sentenced to life in prison. But he should be up for parole in another couple of years."

My sister cried. I was speechless.

Mom had the last word. "Oh, this next weekend," she said brightly, "you're both coming to Walla Walla with me so that you can meet him."

That next weekend we did just that. Mom had filled out all the necessary papers, and my sister and I found ourselves waiting in a room to meet our future stepdad. There were other people in the room too. One couple seemed *very* happy to see each other. Mom told me not to stare. I was 14. I wanted to stare.

Finally, the door opened and in walked a six-foot-two-inch, 265-pound hulk of a man. He had white blond hair, a big blond mustache, a tattoo on his arm, and muscles everywhere. He looked like he was smuggling grapefruits under his shirt.

He walked toward the table where we sat and introduced himself with a smile. His name was Don. He had a pleasant demeanor and seemed eager to meet my sis and me. He told me that he was looking forward to taking me fishing and learning how to play basketball with me. He told my sister that she was beautiful and that he'd always wanted a daughter. Other than the fact that we were meeting in a minimum-security prison complex, everything seemed pretty normal.

We had a pleasant visit that day. Back home, at Mom's urging, we started to write back and forth. It seemed necessary to begin a relationship with this man who would one day move into our house and Mom's heart. Mom and some of our relatives started appealing for an early parole, and it wasn't long before Don was let out to a halfway house in Everett, Washington.

A halfway house is a place where ex-cons learn how to assimilate back into society. They work during the day, and check in and sleep there at night. It's kind of like a boys' dorm in Adventist academies (only less rowdy).

Don was in the halfway house for about a month. He and Mom were married the night he was released. They went on a one-night honeymoon before they came home. All of a sudden we had a new man in the house. A large new man.

We were a model family for about two weeks. Everyone was polite and tolerant, easy to get along with. And then my sister and I found out why Don was put in prison in the first place. We discovered that our new stepfather was critical and negative, with a short fuse that was easy to light. And with the wisdom of teenagers, we felt that it was our duty to keep it lit!

We thought it was kind of fun to provoke him until the vein stuck out of his forehead. You could literally see his pulse in that thing. He would start cussing and fuming, and we'd walk out the door. Now, instead of Mom and Dad arguing, it was Don arguing with his wicked stepchildren. I don't think that my sister ever liked him. I'm not sure if I liked him or not, but it surely was fun to get him mad.

One day my sister and Don were arguing. I remember that it was the middle of the afternoon—Don was never good at holding a steady job—and he took a swing at her. He didn't exactly hit her, but he caught her in the nose with the hard edge of the *TV Guide* he had in his hand. It wasn't long before my sister moved out of the house, with all the implications that held for her life. I stayed home until my high school junior year.

But life at home was pretty tough. I was in the ninth grade when my teacher noticed that I carried some heavy problems around with me. She must have sensed something seriously wrong. I don't know what she saw on this particular day, but she let the class out to play soccer and asked me to stay back and talk with her. She took me into the office, sat me down, and asked me what was wrong. Her kind questioning opened up the floodgates. I must have needed to unload months of pain, for I sat there and told her all the details of what was happening at home. She listened, and her response changed my life.

"I live about a mile away," she told me. "You're welcome at our home anytime. Come after school. Stay the weekend. Whatever you need."

I took her up on it. Weekends, Saturday nights, and any other time I could be there found me with the Tait family. They became my mentors, my lifeline. I had no way of knowing it at the time, but years later their friendship—that they welcomed me and believed in me—would have a dramatic effect on my philosophy of ministry.

It is vitally important that we as adult Christians—no matter what our church affiliation—take personal notice of our young people and take the lead in establishing relationships with them. In other words, don't wait for them to come to you. You seek them out. Go to them.

The Bible even gives us examples of this. Elijah taught Elisha. By word and example, Paul instructed Timothy. God expects us to do the same with the kids and teens in our churches and neighborhoods. Mrs. Tait and her family surely made a difference in my life.

CHAPTER 2

LIFE MOVES ON

Don't get me wrong. As much as my stepfather made my home-life miserable, I dearly loved my mom. She was one person in my life who treated people just as Jesus did. She always loved me and treated me better than I deserved. And I can't tell you how many times she took in friends of mine who couldn't live at home anymore. In fact, my sister and I constantly had friends over. Mom cheerfully cooked for them and cleaned up after them. The bottom line is that she gave me and my friends love and trust. I don't know how she managed it. She knew I was into things that I shouldn't be. She once asked me if the plant I had growing in my closet was legal or not.

I told the truth. "It's not."

Her face clouded with disappointment, but she didn't say much. "Just don't smoke it in the house, OK?" she said.

I didn't.

In a sense, I think that her relationship with my stepfather fell right into Mom's generosity. I also think that Don wanted to be a good person. It's just that a dysfunctional childhood, a basic lack of education, substance abuse, and 18 years of prison all contributed to my stepdad being a bitter, generally unpleasant person. And it made life hard.

Don actually had flashes of kindness. One evening as I sat in the house watching TV, he walked by and dropped a piece of paper in my lap. I picked it up, looked at it, and realized that it was the title to a 1968 Pontiac GTO—a teenager's dream car. I don't know why Don gave it to me. He just did. I said, "Thanks," and that was it—a rare good moment in an otherwise unpleasant existence.

My stepfather's anger and resentfulness kept him from attending our local church. It also estranged him from Mom's family, made enemies of all the people in our neighborhood, and eventually drove him from our family and out of our lives.

I, for one, couldn't wait to get out of the house. When I could finally attend boarding school, I had the best of both worlds. Starting out in the dorm, I eventually became an off-campus student at an Adventist academy only an hour from my home. During the week I stayed at the academy in friends' dorm rooms. Weekends I went home, staying with neighborhood friends or with the Taits. When I did bring friends home with me, it was either to my dad's home (he was in his second marriage by now) or to Mom's. I didn't mind living like this, because I got the best of both worlds: Mom's cooking, and the freedom to be away from home's unhappy situation and—in fact—some of the rules.

I'd looked forward to boarding academy for a number of reasons. For one, I thought I'd finally be with the kind of people who would help me to turn over a new leaf. Those kind *were* there, but I didn't hang out with them. I must have sought out the same kind of friends I had at home. It wasn't long before my experimenting with and abusing illegal substances was heightened by my association with my academy friends. And just as it was back home, some of my friends were just casually into the stuff and others took it way overboard.

Academy also provided a chance for me and my friends to experiment more with practical jokes. Most of them were just dumb little pranks. One winter quarter we took the Christmas tree from the administration building and put it in our room—along with some furniture and the history teacher's office chair.

But the joke I loved the most was a cooperative effort by several of us in the junior class. Somebody had moved a huge old-fashioned refrigerator out of the dorm and left it sitting on the sidewalk outside of one of the entrances. This was too good to ignore. So in the middle of the night a bunch of friends and I hauled it across the academy campus and slid it up an extended ladder onto the top of the art building roof. After spray-painting our class year on it, we sneaked back across campus and into the dorm.

As we walked to class the next morning we saw that the maintenance crew had rented a huge forklift to get the unwanted kitchen appliance off the roof and out of their lives.

Another time during my junior year, my buddies Brad and Troy and I stole a dorm friend's truck and drove to the eastern part of the state to party with some other friends. We left an unsigned note on his bed saying that we'd bring him back a case of his favorite beverage. Before we left, we also cleaned out the dean's closet. Why *his* closet? It held all the confiscated radios and stereos that were contraband in the dorm. Then we drove to Wenatchee and attempted to pawn as many as we could. After all, we needed some cash for traveling.

We were three unruly guys, out for a fairly innocent good time (we thought), unaware that the guy who owned the truck had come back early from weekend leave. His dad was with him. His dad noticed that the truck was gone. His son didn't know where it was. His dad also saw the unsigned note on his son's bed.

The police were called. Some parents in Wenatchee were called. And us? We were as happy as if we'd had good sense, cruising the streets, unaware that anyone knew we were gone . . . until Brad's father started chasing us through the back roads of eastern Washington. We stayed the night at a friend's house, drove back early, and sneaked into the dorm. Brad was kicked out, and took the names of his accomplices home with him. He wouldn't tell; Troy and I were never found out.

Out of all the stupid things I did while in academy, only once was I caught and suspended.

The suspension was for a silly thing; even as an adult I think that.

Again, it was my junior year. The lead singer from a popular rock band had died and, as a tribute to his passing, a group of my friends and I lowered the school flag to half-mast and wore black T-shirts bearing the logo from the local hard-rock station. When the principal saw the shirts and found out what we were up to, he hauled us in one by one and asked that we not wear the shirts at school.

Were we cooperative? Did we want to comply? Of course not.

A couple of us called the local rock station and told them that our school wouldn't allow us to wear their shirts. The station's disc jockey called the principal and interviewed him, edited the interview to make our principal sound like a real idiot (which he was not), and used it as a lead story on the radio station's news. My friends and I got to spend a couple of days away from school for that little escapade.

It didn't matter. My grades were pathetic anyway. I literally didn't learn anything in school. I'm sure I had great teachers. I was just more interested in my social and athletic life than in studying. I flunked junior English. My grades were awful. I didn't even find out I was cleared for graduation until two and a half weeks before we marched.

Some of the teachers did try to reach me; I just brushed them off. My senior Bible teacher made numerous attempts to talk to me about my spiritual life. I wasn't interested. It wasn't that I had anything against God—or the church. I just didn't care. I never responded to an altar call. No teacher, no speaker, no student got through to me. I just didn't care.

I hardly made it through my Bible classes. Like my dad, I was never interested in plugging into a life of faith. I didn't see the need. It just didn't cross my mind as something important for my life. I was happy with the way things were. I couldn't see any reason to stir up my life with a bunch of vague stuff I could never put my finger on.

I graduated from academy—barely—intending to go to college and get serious about life. Once again, I felt it was time to turn over a new leaf. I actually thought I could do it. But once I was at Walla

Walla College, it didn't take long for me to discover that I didn't know how to study. Again, my grades were awful. It could be because I never went to class. Eventually the college administration politely told me that I needed to go somewhere else. Years later, when I was in the theological seminary, I had a meeting with the dean of the school. As he looked over my transcripts, a puzzled look crossed his face. Holding up my Walla Walla College transcript, he asked, "What happened here?"

I'm pretty sure that my highest grade that year was a C—in tennis.

Looking back, I think the worst part of my college experience was that I had no clue that anything was wrong with me. I hung around people who made good grades, who had enough money to get around, and who were pretty clean in the area of substance abuse. They were actually great guys. Not having my life together, I ended up as kind of a mooch (actually, more of a leech) in their lives, and took their friendships for granted. I also had a girlfriend. At the time, I thought I was in love with her. Again, thinking back, I treated her horribly.

As my first year of college ended I came to a terrible realization: *I didn't like myself very much.* I sensed that my life had no direction and that if I didn't smarten up, I'd end up flipping burgers for the rest of my days.

If at First You Don't Succeed

I moved back to Seattle and found a restaurant job that accommodated a school schedule. Community college was easier than private college. That—and the prospect of lifelong failure—produced a lot more effort in my scholastic life. I actually started to learn, and—guess what—my grades went up.

It was about then that I met Marcie, a high school senior who came to work in the restaurant where I worked. She was cute. Friendly. Two weeks before New Year's Eve when I didn't have a date for a concert that I planned to attend, I looked around, considered my options, and asked Marcie.

She said, "Yes."

We had a great time at the concert. The music was loud and energetic (the kind I'm sure my son will never enjoy). At the stroke of midnight the band kept playing, balloons fell from the ceiling, and everyone embraced and kissed. We looked around and, caught up in the excitement, brought the new year in with a kiss too. Something happened during that kiss. Actually, I'm not sure what it was. All I know is that within three weeks Marcie and I had moved in together. Marcie was still in high school, but we were in love . . . for a while.

The first few months of living together were great. And then one day we woke up mad at each other. I think it was because we got to know each other. We loved each other, but we couldn't figure out a way to like each other. The routine would go down something like this. I'd come home from work, and Marcie would start slamming doors and cupboards, all the while giving me a cold shoulder.

"What's wrong?" I'd asked, bewildered.

"Nothing."

"Then why aren't you talking to me? Why are you slamming cupboards?"

"It's me. Don't worry about it."

I've never believed that line. "OK, what's the matter with you?"

"It's not me. It's *you.*"

"OK, what did I do?"

"Nothing. It's me."

It was hard to make very much progress when I couldn't even have a good fight with her. I felt helpless. I was in love with a girl who didn't even like me. I couldn't figure out why she didn't like me. Besides, she stuck around. Maybe she loved me but didn't like me. Maybe she loved me even though I made her mad.

The only solution that I could come up with was to bring up the topic of marriage. So I saved my pennies and purchased a promise ring. Giving a girl a promise ring says "I promise I'll ask you to marry me someday." Accepting it, she promises that she'll say yes. It's kind of like making a decision by forming a subcommittee to form a committee to make a decision.

The ring brought a bit of cheer to the relationship, but it wore off in time. It was sad. I was in and out of school, working in a restaurant trying to make a living, and living with a girl I wasn't sure I liked but intended to marry anyway. Actually, I'd seen few happily married couples in my entire life. I figured that the alternative to being unhappily married was to be lonely, and being unhappily married would be a better alternative than loneliness.

I wasn't happy with my decision, but what else was there to decide? Right? But at age 21 I felt as though my life was swirling down a big cosmic drain. Until one Sunday morning . . .

Stubborn Little Man

I was lounging around the house one Sunday morning, feeling thick-tongued and headachy from the night before, when I heard a knock on our door. I opened the door and saw one of the strangest and most irritating—to me—sights one could see on a Sunday morning.

The man was about five feet five (*if* he'd been wearing high-heeled cowboy boots, which he wasn't). He had a shiny, mostly bald head and a smile almost as big as his face. His leisure suit was shiny with wear, and he held a huge Bible under his arm. He stretched up on his toes when he talked. "Hi!" he said cheerfully. "Are you Mark?"

"Uh, yeah. Who are you?"

"I'm Pastor Dave Yancey. I'm your mom's pastor. Can I come in?"

Before I could answer, he planted his little hand against my chest, moved me aside, and walked into my house. That was a pretty brave move considering he was five feet five, 135 pounds, and I was six feet six, 230 pounds. I followed him into my living room, where we sat down.

"What do you want?" I asked.

He kept smiling. (I still don't like people who smile early on Sunday mornings.) "Mark, you know your mom loves you." I nodded. *Well, yes.* "You know she prays for you every day."

"Yeah, I know," I said.

"Mark, we have some meetings coming up at her church."

"What kind of meetings?" I asked, instantly suspicious.

"Prophecy seminar meetings. They're about Daniel and Revelation."

I remembered prophecy seminars. I'd seen the division this stuff had caused in my family, and heard enough in school to know that I wasn't interested. "Well, you know," I told Pastor Dave, "I really don't want to attend any church meetings."

"OK," he said with a smile. He got up and left.

What a strange little man, I thought.

The next Sunday about the same time, I heard a knock on my door. It was Pastor Dave.

We went through the same routine. "Mark, your mom loves you. She's praying for you. We've got these meetings at the church."

"I'm not interested," I told him. Again.

Again, he just smiled and left. Either Pastor Dave had a short memory or he was more persistent than I wanted him to be.

Five Sundays in a row he came to my house and went through the same routine. Finally I kept him outside on the stoop and asked, "What is it going to take to get you to stop knocking on my door?"

"Come to the meetings."

"I'm not going to come to your stupid meetings!" I tried to sound tough.

"Then I'm not going to quit bothering you." He did sound tough.

I decided to try a different tactic. "OK, I'll make you a deal."

"Shoot," he said. (I felt like shooting.)

"What if I come to the first meeting? I'll get there early, and I'll leave when it's finished. If I like the meeting I'll come to the next one. If I don't, I won't be obligated to come back. If I promise to do that, will you stop bothering me?"

He stuck out his hand. "Deal."

He left. He was also true to his word. The only time he contacted me after that was to call to remind me that the meetings would begin the next evening.

The dreaded day came. I'd promised. There was no honorable way out of it. I was getting dressed to go when Marcie got home from work.

"Where are you going?" she asked.

"I'm going to a meeting at my mom's church."

She started laughing. "No, seriously, where are you going?"

When I finally convinced her, she decided to come too. She'd been to church about twice in her life. We were early, and walked in together. We were greeted warmly, handed a couple of Bibles, and directed into the sanctuary. We sat toward the back and waited.

Right Direction, Wrong Reason

It felt strange to walk into the church that I'd attended as a child. I was familiar with the layout, and the people were still friendly, but I wasn't comfortable walking in. I had visions of old ladies pinching my cheek and saying, "I remember you when you were just *thiiiiis* tall." I felt even more uncomfortable because I didn't want my mom to get any ideas in her head about me becoming a permanent fixture in the place.

We sat in the back wondering what we'd gotten ourselves into. As people started to make their way into the sanctuary, I noticed something that made me wonder. I saw couples that obviously belonged there (I remembered some of them from years before) walking down the aisle holding hands. Some of them were talking and laughing. Some of them had children who seemed to enjoy being with their parents. All that was right out of a Disney movie. How could these people be so happy? How could they be married and be this happy? It just didn't make sense to me. It was just an act, right?

Pretty soon the meeting started. A woman got up and sang a solo. The style of music and the way she sang made both Marcie and me laugh. Marcie wasn't familiar with church music, and I'd never particularly liked it. Then somebody got up and welcomed everyone, and made some announcements about the rest of the meetings. I wasn't planning to attend, so I didn't listen. Finally the evangelist was introduced. As he began talking, my mind started to wander. I looked at all of the people sitting around us, all the happy families. Right in front of us sat the head elder of the church, his wife, and kids. They seemed to adore him. I remembered that their names were Ron and Cita. I couldn't get over how in love they seemed. And after all this time! Ron kept his arm around her, and they nodded and smiled at each other a lot.

I felt trapped. Here I was, sitting in church next to a girl I loved but didn't like. I had very little education and was trapped in a dead-end job. I just wanted out. But how?

Then a strange thought hit me—the perfect plan to break up with my girlfriend and possibly get a new lease on life. I don't know where the thought came from, for I surely wouldn't blame it on God. But it was my first thought in a while that didn't die of loneliness, and those were rare. Actually it was more of an epiphany.

I'd spent enough time in church and in church school to know that one of the "don'ts" in the Christian life was fornication. Christians were not supposed to live together "in sin." Suddenly it all made perfect sense. *If I become a Christian, Marcie will have to move out. And that will make it a lot easier to break up with her.* The idea was a stroke of brilliance. Maybe not theologically inspired, but certainly a stroke of brilliance.

I picked up my Bible and caught up to where the evangelist was, and pretended I was riveted to every word. When the meeting finished, I looked at Marcie and said, "Wow, that was great, wasn't it?"

She looked at me and said, "Uh, no."

We attended every meeting. We didn't miss one. I was on a foolproof path and not about to get off. Finally, at the close of one of the meetings the evangelist made an altar call. He said that anyone who wanted to be baptized should walk down the aisle and meet him in the front of the church. I didn't even hesitate. When I reached the front, the little irritating pastor who had knocked on my door 100 times raced down the platform stairs, buried his head in my chest, and hugged me for all he was worth. When the meeting was over, he prayed with me and the other individuals who had followed my lead, then dismissed us.

Marcie and I had an interesting drive home. At first it was silent. Then it got real loud. "Why in the world did you have to walk down front tonight? What were you thinking?"

I didn't know what to say. I had a plan, and I was sticking to it. I decided to take the direct route and just spill the beans. "I've decided to become a Christian. When are you moving out?"

"I'm not moving out!" she shrieked. "Why do I have to move out?"

"Duh! I'm becoming a Christian! Christians don't live together without being married. Everybody knows that. You have to move out!" I was sticking to the plan.

Marcie was furious and deeply hurt. As soon as we got home she called her dad and asked him to bring his truck and help her move. "Why do you have to become a Christian and mess everything up? Why can't we just have it like it was?"

I didn't want it like it was. I *wasn't* sure that I wanted to become a Christian, but I was sure that I didn't want it like it was. She moved out. All of a sudden I was at home alone and headed toward baptism. Kind of an unsettling feeling. Again, not theologically correct, but baptism seemed like a logical way out of a life that didn't seem to be going anywhere fast.

As I've gotten older and have reflected on how I've lived my life, one of the greatest regrets I have is not what I've done to myself, but what I've done to hurt other people. Sometimes—too often—my being a moron seemed to include hurting the people around me. When I was younger, I lived like I was an island unto myself. Now I realize that everything we do affects those around us. Breaking up with Marcie was a lot like going through a divorce. And since I was the one who wanted the change, the hurt I inflicted upon her must have been awful. I wish they made adhesive bandages for that kind of pain, because as I look back on my life I left more than a little emotional pain in my wake. But at the time I wasn't as concerned with Marcie's pain as I was about the direction my life was going.

I had to make a change. How could I drift into marriage with someone who didn't even like me? I'd set it up so she'd have to leave. And she had.

With Marcie gone, I felt like I had to stick to my plan for credibility's sake, so I continued attending the meetings. I paid attention. And it's funny, but I found that as I listened to the speaker, the things he taught made a lot of sense. I actually became convinced that the evangelist was teaching truth. Indeed, I decided, *if* there was a church out there that followed the Bible as closely as possible, it was the Seventh-day Adventist Church. After the meetings were over, I didn't have any doubt that this was the church I would join—if I were to join a church.

The evening that the meetings were over, Pastor Dave called on my home again. "Mark, when can I come over and study the Bible with you?"

What!

"Pastor Dave, I didn't miss any of the meetings. I went to all of them. I studied the Bible every night for the past several weeks. I know all that stuff now."

Pastor Dave responded with wisdom from above. "Mark, I know we've convinced you. Now I'd like to convert you? God's got your brain, but He'd like your heart."

I had no idea what he was talking about, but we scheduled an appointment for that next Tuesday evening. He came over, opened his Bible, and started studying from the book of John. It wasn't too long before I saw that there was a difference between being convinced and being converted. Pastor Dave taught me about grace and the cross. He taught me that God was madly in love with me and had gone to great lengths of personal pain and sacrifice to win me back into communion with Him.

One night when we were studying the cross from the disciple Peter's perspective, something happened. All of a sudden I realized where I stood with God. I understood who He is and who I am. I saw myself as Peter saw himself after denying Jesus. I felt that look; the look Jesus gave Peter after he'd sworn he didn't know Him, and then the rooster crowed.

For the first time in my life I knew who I was, and more important, who God thought I was. It was painful, but it was a good thing. I broke down in tears and started to weep. Pastor Dave patted my shoulder and said, "It's OK; it's OK."

I looked at him through tear-misted eyes and said, "How could I have missed it all these years? I used to go to church. They taught me this stuff in church school. My mom taught me this stuff, but somehow I missed it. I know they taught it, but I missed it."

Again, I'm sure that God gave Pastor Dave the right words at the right time. "Maybe God needed to take some extra time to prepare you for *this* moment. Sometimes He leads us down the long road to conversion for a reason." I didn't know the reason, but I surely was grateful to know that God was indeed leading me.

Underwater Surprise

Pastor Dave asked me if I felt comfortable being baptized that month. I was a bit hesitant because I worked in a grocery store and they often asked me to work Saturdays. I knew this was a conflict of interest if I were to become an SDA. I told Pastor Dave that I'd pray about it and tell him what I was going to do.

I did make it a matter of prayer. I was pretty new at the whole prayer thing, so my prayer was probably pretty crude. It went something like "Listen, God, if You want me to be a Seventh-day Adventist, then I'm going to need a job." Not very eloquent, but sincere.

It was about a week later that a fellow from across the street walked into the store to buy some lunch. He'd been in a hundred times and was always friendly. We knew each other on a first-name basis. This particular day he looked at me and said, "Hey, you're a pretty friendly guy. How would you like to work for my television station?"

"Are you serious? What would I do?"

He explained that I would kind of be a gofer, doing all sorts of things for both the radio and television sections of a local ABC affiliate. Then I remembered my dilemma. "I can't work on Saturdays," I told him. "Is that OK?"

"Hey, I'm Jewish. Half the people at the station are Jewish. Sabbath is not a problem. You can come to temple with me this Friday night."

That next week I started my new job. That next Sabbath I was baptized.

My baptism was a trip. I got to the church, and Pastor Dave had me go into a room and change into my baptismal robe. He came in soon after and changed into his robe. I noticed a vast difference in how his fit him and how mine fit me. (Just a note to the reader: If you ever find yourself designing baptismal robes for a living, please remember tall people!) I felt like I was wearing a miniskirt. I would have been real nervous if the robe hadn't had little weights sewn into the hem. At least it wouldn't float up in some embarrassing way.

Finally Pastor Dave and I stood at the door, ready to enter the water on the other side. I was curious. "Pastor Dave, I'm six feet six and 230 pounds. You're five feet five and 135 pounds. How are you going to get me out of the water?"

He looked at me with a sneaky little smile on his face. "Don't worry about it. I've got a secret."

He opened the door and we walked down the stairs and into the water. He turned me so that I was facing the congregation and said some nice things about our studies together. Finally he said a prayer, put his hand over my nose and mouth, and lowered me into the water.

Lowering me was easy. Getting me back up was a challenge. His little secret turned out to be a knee, placed firmly in the middle of my back, in order to start me up in the right direction. Now, I don't know if anyone has ever kneed you in the middle of the back, unexpectedly, underwater. It took me, and my lungs (now on the other side of his knee), by surprise. I gulped and shot up out of the water gasping and wheezing.

One of the people sitting on the front row was a newly baptized Adventist, right out of a Pentecostal church. She must have assumed that my wheezing was the Spirit descending, because she stood up, raised her hand in the air, and shouted, "Glory!"

What started out as an attempt to break up with my girlfriend ended with my converted heart and a new birth. My motives were anything but pure. God's motives were always on task, and always pure. I guess in the long run my motives somehow fell into God's plan. Somehow, He was there waiting so that at just the right time He could give me the chance to answer His call. I didn't even know that I was listening for a call.

A Weird Haircut and an Empty Youth Chapel

Soon after I was baptized the church put me in charge of the youth department. The church had a beautiful youth chapel, evidence of a once thriving youth program, but I'm not sure you could call what we had a "department." It was barely a small group. My first Sabbath as youth leader was a challenge to say the least. The program was supposed to start at 9:30. By 10:00 five young people were sitting in the back seats, looking down, and playing some electronic game. Whatever they were doing, they surely weren't interested in what I had to say to them.

Week after week I'd show up and teach Sabbath school. As week followed week the numbers started to increase until we had a pretty healthy youth group. I was becoming a part of my church and loving it. I had no idea that being a part of a biblical community could be so fulfilling. I loved my church, and my church loved me.

This was in the early eighties when certain styles of clothing and hair dress were "in." In keeping with the fad, I had a haircut that was unusual for someone deeply involved in a local Seventh-day Adventist church. But it wasn't my spiked hair that concerned some of the folks at church. It was the tail. I had let a strand of hair (called "tails" in the eighties) about six inches long grow down my back. I hadn't given my tail much thought until during a church business meeting one of our local elders asked me when I was going to get a haircut.

I told him that he couldn't pay me enough to cut my hair. He suggested that he could. At the end of our meeting, he stood up and announced to those in attendance that we were going to have an auction. What was up for auction? My tail. The money would be donated to the youth program.

Before I knew it, people were bidding for the right to tomahawk my tail. I'm not sure what the final bid was—more than the price of a good haircut—but our head elder, Ron Sakkariason, won the bid. He took a big pair of scissors and cut off my tail. He stood there, scissors in one hand, and held it up, whooping like a Comanche in an old Western and waving it in the air. I had to laugh. Now I even looked like a Seventh-day Adventist, or at least what one was supposed to look like back then.

CHAPTER 3

I'M NOT LOOKING FOR A DATE, SORT OF

When I finally decided to become a Christian I wanted to clean up all of the problem areas of my life. Thus, I tried to deal with a lot of lifestyle issues, changing my behavior in a lot of areas that I wasn't satisfied with. I wasn't trying to do any of this to make myself more likable to God or anything; I just wanted to have my life completely turned around and going in a positive direction in as many areas as my will and God's power could muster.

Unfortunately, when we poor humans attempt to clean up ourselves, on our own agenda, God's agenda gets left by the wayside. This was the case when I made a solemn vow to God about my dating life. I told God—and my close friends at church—that I was going to take a long break from women. I figured that so far in my life women were bad for me. Or that I was bad for them. Something was bad, and it had to do with me and women. So I made my solemn pledge and stuck to it for almost a year. I didn't go on one date (not that anyone wanted to date me). I didn't even ask a girl out.

I was nearing the life of a true monk, chaste and pure. And then one Sabbath morning I saw her—standing alone in the church foyer. Like Eve, wandering near the tree of temptation, I asked one of the greeters who she was.

"She's the new teacher at the elementary school," the greeter said, nudging me in the ribs. "She's single, too." *Wink-wink.*

I was offended by the mere inference that I would even think of breaking my promise to God. I sneaked around the corner and stared at the newcomer, telling myself, "I'm not interested. I'm not interested. I'M NOT INTERESTED!"

The next Friday night the new girl, Wendy, tried out for a part in the church choir. We were working on an Easter cantata in which the soloists had to audition for parts. While different people took their turns at this particular solo almost everyone else was chatting in the back of the room. Then Wendy started to sing. One by one, everyone stopped talking and started listening to the best voice that any of us had ever heard. I was in love. I didn't know her, but I was in love.

After practice I approached her. "Hey, I've got a bunch of people coming over to my house for lunch after church tomorrow. Would you like to come over?"

She looked up at me and said, "I'm sorry; I have a boyfriend. I'm not interested."

I panicked and lied. "Uh, I'm not looking for a relationship. There's going to be a big group. It's just a chance for you to get to know some people your age. So what do you think?"

She was still tentative. "Well, OK. I'll come over."

I couldn't wait for church to end. After it was finally over, Wendy had me follow her home, where she parked and left her car. Then she rode with me to my house, where there were several people our age already cooking and visiting. After we ate, somehow Wendy and I ended up in my backyard, sitting on the grass and talking. I'd never experienced communication with a woman like that. It was beautiful. We just talked, shared, and laughed about life in general. Wendy had a willow switch in her hand and was wiggling it around on the grass when a cat jumped over the fence and started chasing it. She was delighted. "I love animals!" she said.

I suddenly developed a deep love for critters. "*I* love animals too." (What a coincidence!)

Everyone stayed into the evening, visiting and playing games. Finally, around 10:00 people started to leave. Wendy looked at me and asked if I'd take her home. When we pulled into her driveway I asked her if I could come in and get a drink of water. She fell for it and let me in. Usually I'm a gulper. On this night I was a sipper. I sat on her couch, and we started to talk again. Before we knew it, it was 2:00 a.m. Wendy looked at the clock and said, "What are you still doing here? Get out!"

I got up to leave, and then blurted out one of the stupidest things I've ever said. I looked at her and said, "I'm convinced that you are the woman I'm going to marry."

She just stared at me. Finally she spoke. "Are you nuts? I've only known you for one day. Marry you? I would *never* marry you. I would have to know someone for at least two years before I would even *think* of marrying him. Please leave now!"

I grabbed a calendar off the wall and flipped it ahead five months to August. I pointed to the middle of August and said, "I will be married to you on or before August 18." And then I ran out the door.

Wendy and I were married August 4, 1985. Now, I normally wouldn't recommend a five-month courtship. I don't think I would have even recommended it for myself. But at the writing of this book, we've been married for nearly 16 years now, and I couldn't imagine having it any better.

With such a short engagement there wasn't much time for wedding plans. One thing was for sure, there was going to be a lot of music in it. Wendy is an incredible musician who loves music as she loves life. Immediately she started planning the most musical wedding ever! Then she broke the news to me—she had written a song that we were to sing to each other.

There are few things that strike fear in me the way singing in front of people does. I think I sound fine in the shower, but when I sing in front of people, any people, my throat feels like its being squeezed by a vice. Nevertheless, I was to sing to my bride at my wedding.

The ceremony took place at the church where I was baptized.

The guests were all in their seats. Wendy's first and second grade class lined the aisle holding candles. The music started to play; I stood up front with my best man. The back doors swung open and there she was—and there I went.

As soon as I saw her I started to sob. I'm not even sure why, but my face was leaking like a sieve. Of course, I had no hanky. My best man had no hanky (the one job a best man has, he failed at, miserably). So when my bride and her father finally made it down the aisle, I had only my hand and my sleeve to alleviate my moisture problem.

When the processional stopped I was to walk down the platform steps, get a microphone, and start singing the first part of our song. Wendy was doing great until she saw that I was blubbering. She started crying, which made me cry even more. The music began, I picked up the microphone, choking on my tears.

It's already difficult to sing when you're afraid to sing in front of people. It's even more difficult to sing when you are dripping onto the microphone. We made it through the song, walked up the stairs to the pastor, and prepared to say our vows. The pastor took one look at us and started crying too. He had one hanky. We shared.

It turned out to be a beautiful wedding. The music was wonderful, the cake was good, and we didn't get electrocuted by any wet microphones.

After the wedding Wendy and I took our already packed belongings and headed up to the Canadian border for our honeymoon and the beginning of our new life together. We honeymooned in Victoria, British Columbia, and had a grand time. Life couldn't have been much better.

To the Mountains

Immediately after our honeymoon Wendy and I left for Bella Coola, British Columbia to work for a little Adventist academy in the mountains. For four years I was a boys' dean and taught Bible. They were four of the best years of my life. I was working with teenagers (and getting paid for it), I was learning how to be a married person, and I was learning how to be a Christian all at the same time.

It was really a case of knowing the right people that took us to Bella Coola. Wendy's father is a dentist who started the little junior academy with the British Columbia Conference's blessings in the midseventies. By the mideighties, when we were married, it had become a healthy little school that needed a Bible teacher. What a trip.

Wendy and I first moved into a little cabin on the edge of an orchard on her parents' property. I'll never forget my experience that first morning. I woke up, threw on some sweat pants, and walked out the back door. As I stood on the our back porch admiring the view, I saw the strangest thing. About 50 feet away I saw a huge black dog eating some fallen apples. I yelled back into the house, "Hey, Wendy, there's a big black dog eating apples in our backyard. What kind of dog eats apples?"

"That's not a dog," she said. "It's a bear."

I wheeled around and took a second look. Sure enough, there was a bear in my backyard. My wife grew up in Bella Coola. She thought this was normal. I ran in the house and hid under the bed.

Bella Coola Adventist Academy was the most unique Adventist school I'd ever seen. In order to gain their physical education credit, all the students took part in monthly backpacking, camping, and orienteering trips. For four years I got to hike, camp out in, and climb around the coastal mountains of British Columbia. And they paid me for it.

When I ended up in the dorm as the boys' dean, I really fell in love with my job. I loved the everyday interaction with the guys, the faculty and staff, and the church members in that little town. I ended up being the boys' dean and Bible teacher, and depending on the year, the choral director, the drama team director, and the work program coordinator. Believe it or not, I think I worked the least of any of the staff members at that precious little school.

It's been a lot of years since Wendy and I worked in Bella Coola, but we still keep in touch with many of our students. Every few years or so we go back and hike in the Tweedsmuir National Park. It's a wonderful trip that consists of roughly 26 miles of hiking and five large lakes of canoeing and portaging.

But it wasn't the beauty of the mountains that made it so hard to leave Bella Coola. It was the people.

White-water Pastor

After several years there, I thought it would be a good idea to get an education, and decided to go back to Walla Walla and finish college. Just about then the Washington Conference of Seventh-day Adventists called me and asked if I'd like to be the youth pastor in a Seattle-area church. We struck a deal, and I became a Seventh-day Adventist youth pastor and full-time university student. I went to Seattle Pacific University by day and spent my nights and weekends in youth ministry.

My new church was also my old church. It was the church that Mom went to when I was a kid, the church that I came back to for my baptism, and my first church as a youth pastor. I was embraced by the membership and had a wonderful learning experience in ministry.

One of the most unusual ministries of this church was a rafting ministry. On summer weekends we'd host groups on different rivers in western Washington. Typically we'd have a nature float on Sabbath—actually, the nature float usually turned into a huge water fight—and then a white-water experience on Sunday. Many times we invited a guest speaker to minister to the group and to challenge us spiritually. They were very full weekends.

We were enriched spiritually. We grew socially. And white-water rafting was an education. At times it was also frightening.

One of my frightening but cherished experiences was the weekend that my conference treasurer, Roy Wesson, came along. A wonderful man, just ready for retirement, he happened to join our group on the weekend that we were training new guides. Also joining us on the trip was my sister. Lori was very afraid of white-water rafting, but on this particular weekend determined to face her fear and come along.

We all got into the raft, and I explained that we were going to be led by two guides-in-training. I said that I was going to be along, but I wasn't going to say anything. I was going to let the guides do the guiding while I enjoyed the ride.

The first serious white water one comes to when rafting the Wenatchee River is called Satan's Eyeball. There's a reason for that name. If you don't hit the rapid straight on with some momentum, it can suck you and your raft into a hydraulic, flip your raft, and drown everybody.

So the key is to hit it with momentum on a pretty straight line.

We, of course, hit it sideways with no momentum at all. The hydraulic started sucking. It sucked my conference treasurer out. It sucked my sister and her friend out. It tried to flip the whole raft. It didn't. We saved the raft from flipping, got out of the hydraulic's grip, and started floating down the river. We quickly retrieved my sister and her friend into the raft, but we couldn't find Elder Wesson anywhere. Talk about a feeling of panic! Finally we located him—about 50 yards down the river, heading right toward a dam.

It was all we could do to speed-paddle downriver and save his life. I'll never forget it. Elder Wesson had such a good humor about him. He was the only person in our raft who wasn't wearing a wet suit, and the river was cold. But he had a grin on his face as we hauled him into the raft. "I thought you'd never get here!" he said.

My paycheck came on time that month! Believe it or not.

The Life of a Pastor's Wife

When she was in college Wendy had an awful time with the theology majors. Blond hair, plays the piano, and sings . . . you do the math. Without knowing it, Wendy was a theology major's dream. Unfortunately, she never wanted to marry a pastor. I'm not sure why she was avoiding all us pastor types, but I think that whatever she thought life with a pastor would be like didn't happen in our marriage.

Most of our friends credit Wendy with being the most patient woman they have ever met. I resent that. I agree with it, but I resent it. The fact is that without knowing it, Wendy married a man who has a huge need for fun. I love getting a good reaction. I love to laugh at a good reaction. Sometimes, though, I wonder if Wendy is having as much fun as I am.

One of the most terrible things I've ever done to her was the time I made her think that our TV was possessed. While in seminary we rented a huge house right off the campus of Andrews University. In the basement of that house was a little room that we put our TV in and also used as an office. One day Wendy was sitting in our lounge chair and watching television. What she didn't know was that I had purchased a new remote control for the TV and was standing just outside the almost-closed door.

As she sat watching, I stood outside the door and changed the channel. She changed it back. I changed it again. She changed it back. I pushed the channel changer down and started surfing from channel to channel. She finally just turned it off. When I turned it back on again and shot the volume through the roof, she jumped up, screamed, and ran for the door. Just as she got there I opened it up and yelled, "RAWWWWW!"

She pounded my chest until she collapsed in laughter. She was sure that Satan had somehow gotten into our television.

One of the first points of contention that Wendy and I had, had very little to do with me being a pastor. Instead, it had to do with how we were raised. She was raised a vegetarian. I was only a vegetarian when my mom got a veggie bee in her bonnet. So I wasn't a vegetarian when we first met.

Wendy isn't a vegetarian for her health. She's a vegetarian because she loves animals more than she loves people. We'd be sitting in a restaurant, and before I could eat my first bite of chicken Wendy would look at me with a sad face and say, "How could you eat something that once had a mother?"

To which I'd always reply, "Well, I think Jesus ate meat." She swore up and down that Jesus turned all of the meat He ate into a soy product before it even met His lips.

One Thanksgiving we had my family over, and everyone contributed to the meal. Dad was in charge of the stuffing. What Wendy didn't know, and what I had completely forgotten, was that one of the central ingredients in Dad's stuffing was pork.

It wasn't until we were eating that I remembered. Wendy leaned over and whispered to me, "This is the best stuffing I've ever tasted in my life."

I looked down at her half-eaten portion of stuffing, leaned over as she was chewing her next bite, and whispered, "Oink, oink."

I'll never forget the look on her face. Not wanting to offend my dad (whom she loves dearly), she quickly deposited the masticated remains of Dad's stuffing out of her mouth and into a napkin . . . and onto my lap.

Our life together hasn't been all jokes though. We've had 16 wonderful years in ministry together. We've been so fortunate as to travel together and experience life as a couple in love. We've walked under a full moon around the Colosseum in Italy. We've helped to build orphanages in developing countries. We've ministered together in the former Soviet Union, and been all over North America to camp meetings, colleges, and academies doing what we love to do best—sharing the gospel through the gifts and talents that God has blessed us with.

Phone Call of a Lifetime

Life couldn't have been better. I was married to the girl of my dreams, doing a job that seemed more like a great hobby, and experiencing as full a life as anyone could ever wish for.

And then one wonderful Friday night the phone rang. The female voice on the other end asked for Mark Witas. I told her that I was Mark.

"My name is Jeanette Bruner," she continued. "I'm calling from San Jose, California. Twenty-nine years ago I had a little boy and gave him up for adoption. I think you might be my son."

I was stunned. I said, "Could you please hold?" I ran down the hall into my office and found my adoption papers. I'd never really read them, so when I got back on the phone I looked on the document and said, "This document calls me 'Baby Judson.' Does the name 'Judson' mean anything to you?"

The woman took a deep breath. "Judson is my maiden name. You're my son."

She had my attention. "Tell me the story. How did it happen?"

"Well, I was a freshman and he was a senior in college. He was big, athletic, and drove a Corvette. I thought I was in love, so one weekend we decided to go away and spend a few days together on the beach. In one night I lost my virginity and became pregnant."

"That's a lot to do in one night," I said. "What did he say when you told him you were pregnant?"

"He didn't want to have anything to do with the situation. And I didn't want my parents to find out, so I moved to another city and found a family that took me in. I had you in secret."

And all this time I thought I was from the baby store!

"Why didn't you tell your parents?" I asked her. "It seems like your parents would have been the first people you would have gone to when you were in trouble."

She said, "You don't understand. My parents were very strict."

"What do you mean, strict?"

"Well, they were strict in a religious sense. Have you ever heard of the Seventh-day Adventists?"

I hesitated, then decided to play my cards close to my chest. "I've heard of them."

"Well, my parents were Seventh-day Adventists. My dad used to teach at La Sierra College. I never liked being a Seventh-day Adventist. So I relinquished you to the state of California." (She never knew that I was in foster care.) "Anyway, tell me what you do for a living."

The irony was killing me. "I'm a Seventh-day Adventist pastor."

I don't remember her reaction, but I think she thought I was joking.

"I'm not kidding. I'm a Seventh-day Adventist pastor." *I couldn't even believe I was saying that.* I can imagine what it must have sounded like to her.

After the shock wore off, we talked for a couple of hours about our lives. I found out that my whole biological family is Seventh-day Adventist. Both of her sisters and her mother are Adventists. Unfortunately, I never got to meet my grandfather. The only person in my immediate birth family who isn't an Adventist is my mom. At the time, she and her husband were attending a Unitarian church. When she told me that, I couldn't resist. I asked her, "What do you get when you cross a Jehovah's Witness with a Unitarian?"

She played along. "What?"

"Someone who knocks on your door for no apparent reason." Thankfully, she laughed.

At the end of our conversation she told me that she contacted me because she just needed to know that I was healthy and happy. She thanked me for letting her talk with me and then acted as though she was going to hang up.

I couldn't just leave it at that. "Wait a minute. You're not just going to hang up, are you? When can we meet? When can I see you?"

"You would like to meet me?" she asked.

"Of course I would. I haven't seen you in 29 years, and frankly, I don't even remember the last time I saw you."

She laughed. "When would you like to see me?"

My birthday was in two weeks. She knew that. She had remembered every January 31 for the past 28 years. This year would be no exception. I couldn't think of a more appropriate reunion time. We decided to have her fly up to Seattle and meet me on my twenty-ninth birthday. I couldn't wait.

Meeting Again for the First Time

For 29 years I had what I considered a good life. My mom and dad had always loved me and treated me well. And I loved my family—Mom, Dad, and sister—with all my heart. They are my family. It never entered my mind to try to find my birth parents. I had been blessed with a good family that took care of me, so why go looking, right? The fact that I had been found—I didn't even know that I was lost!—took me by surprise. But I was really excited about meeting the person who had brought me into this world.

The day came. We'd arranged to meet at the airport, and I was worse than a girl on her first date. I changed my clothes about four times and spent way too much time looking in the mirror. When I was ready to go, I had a childhood friend pick me up in his limo. He had a limousine service, and when he found out about my birth mother he offered to take me in one of his limos. I thought it would be a nice touch. I wanted my mom to know that Adventist clergy didn't fare too badly.

We got to the airport, and it was a madhouse. The Gulf War was in full swing, so the airport had heightened security. And they were shooting airport scenes for the movie *Sleepless in Seattle*. It couldn't have been more crowded.

I had just walked into the terminal when I looked up and saw her. Our eyes connected, and we fell into each other's arms. We just stood there holding each other for a long time. Neither of us felt the need to say anything. We just needed to hold each other.

Finally we parted, and she looked up at me with tears in her eyes. "You're beautiful," she said. (Her tears must have blurred her vision.)

"Were you able to see me or hold me at all?" I asked.

"I couldn't."

"The doctors wouldn't let you?"

"No, that wasn't it. I knew that if I even looked at you, I wouldn't be able to give you up. I just thought the best thing to do was to relinquish you. So I couldn't look."

We made our way out to the limo. My friend pretended to be my personal driver. (I assured my birth mother that I hadn't been dipping into the collection plate.) We sat in the back of the limo as my friend drove us around the city and then to some sites around the area. Finally we got to my home and spent some time looking at baby pictures and sharing stories.

That evening, some church members had a birthday party planned for me. My mom had never been around a group of church members that were so insane. We had a ball. Collectively, they gave me a bunch of boxer shorts with different designs and messages on them and made me promise that I'd wear them when I preached. My mom said, "This isn't how I remember church members acting the last time I was in church." I was thankful for that.

The next day was Sabbath, and as I stood up in my church to preach, my mother and my birth mother sat next to each other holding hands. I have no idea what I spoke about.

At the end of the weekend we parted ways, having spent three days bonding as mother and son. Since then I have been incorporated into the Judson family, and it's as if I'd been there all along. Wendy and I have spent vacations with my new family and have fallen in love with all of them. I've even had the privilege of baptizing a couple of my cousins. What a life!

At the time of this writing, it's been 10 years since I met my birth mother. She has become a best friend, a mom, and an example to me on how to treat other people. There isn't a week that goes by that we don't talk at least a couple of times on the phone. She loves me as if she raised me—maybe even more. And I don't know that I could love her more, or be more proud of her.

My "Aha" Moment

The night I received "the call" had me so riled up I couldn't sleep, so I went into my office and decided to read myself to sleep. Usually that doesn't take long for a man with my attention span, but this particular night I stumbled across a section of the Bible that hit me like a two-by-four. Normally I'd think that I stumbled onto this text entirely by accident, but I know that God's hand guided me this night, as it had been guiding me all along.

I somehow found my way to Psalm 139. As I read the verses in this psalm, it dawned on me for the first time in my life that God had actually planned on me, even before I was born. In other words, *I was no accident.* Listen to what the psalmist says, beginning with verse 13: "For you created my inmost being; you knit me together in my mother's womb. I praise you because I am fearfully and wonderfully made; your works are wonderful, I know that full well. My frame was not hidden from you when I was made in the secret place. When I was woven together in the depths of the earth, your eyes saw my unformed body. *All the days ordained for me were written in your book before one of them came to be"* (verses 13-16, NIV).

This just floored me. It completely ruined my "life happens" philosophy and gave me a new paradigm. All my days were written in God's book before one of them came to be? That means that I was no accident. I was planned for. God planned for me and had a purpose for my life before I was even born. Then I found Ephesians 1. It says that God had plans for me before He created the world. Do you know what this means?

It means that there is no such thing as an illegitimate child. No such thing as a bastard. There is not a person born into this world who was not planned for, even looked forward to with anticipation, by their Creator. This also means that even when I was at my worst, God was with me and had a plan for me. It didn't matter where I was or what I was doing—God was there, waiting for me to discover His plan for my life.

The fact that God plans for each one of us, that none of us are accidents, has led my wife and me down the path of parenthood in a very special way. On June 19, 1997, a little life was born to a young unmarried couple that didn't have the ability or the desire to raise him. God led these young people to contact Wendy and me, and we adopted their baby boy into our family. Our son is the light of our life. Adopting, loving, and nurturing Cole has only heightened my certainty that God plans for us, loves us, and nurtures us as we are adopted into His family. I'm as certain as I've ever been that my son is not an illegitimate child. He was planned for, just as I was planned for.

If these things are true of me, I know they are true of you, also. You are no cosmic accident. God had a plan for you before the creation of the world. He just can't wait for you to discover that plan! He can't wait to reveal to you how you fit into His world, His church, and into His plan for the world. *You*—not the preacher—are an integral part of God's game plan in this great controversy between the good and evil that we call life. Your life, your choices, your willingness to follow His lead, has been planned for. And when you choose to discover and follow God's plan, your life and the lives of those around you will never be the same.

CHAPTER 4

VALUABLE YOU (THE THEOLOGY OF A NEW PARADIGM)

It's My Party; I Can Cry if I Want To

When I was a kid my neighborhood was known for its birthday parties. It seemed that every parent tried to outdo the others, and Mom made sure that my tenth birthday was a blowout. I invited all of my school and neighborhood friends, and my mom took us to a pizza parlor that ran old, silent Laurel and Hardy movies. When we were stuffed with pizza, we came back home and played games. Only then did I open my presents. It was a pretty good party.

Of all the gifts I got that day, the best was from Mom and Dad. After everyone had left, Dad walked over to the closet, pulled out a long slim package, and handed it to me.

Opening it, I was thrilled to see a single-pump Daisy BB gun. My dad eagerly showed me how to load it and shoot it in our backyard. We set up old milk cartons full of water and shot them full of holes and made a target out of an old garbage can lid. It was great fun.

One bright early spring day my friends and I decided to take my air rifle and do some target practice. First we shot at some cartons and bottles in my backyard. When that got boring, we started looking around the neighborhood for other things to shoot. My next-door neighbors had an above-ground swimming pool with an aluminum siding "wall" and a plastic liner inside. We thought it would be fun to see what kind of noise the BBs made when they hit the siding, the water, and whatever else was in my neighbor's yard.

We did that for a while, then eventually put the gun away and left to do something else.

The next day our neighbor, Mr. Enzie, knocked on our door. It seems that the BBs that struck his pool did more than make noise. They also punctured the lining, creating 10 or so small leaks in the aluminum siding. Basically, my $30 BB gun had ruined his $300 pool. It wasn't long before my friends' folks were calling my parents, informing them that I wasn't allowed to associate with their children for a couple of weeks, and I was to stay away from their property.

I was ostracized from my own neighborhood! For two weeks I couldn't even call my friends. The whole neighborhood ganged up on me. And to make things worse, the next day I had my gun taken away from me for accidentally shooting my sister in the hand. I didn't see what the big deal was; it took the doctor only10 minutes to locate the BB and get it out.

When I thought my life had hit rock bottom, something even worse happened. My neighbors—the ones with the leaky swimming pool—sent out invitations for their son's birthday party. It was in 10 days, and I was the only kid in a 10-mile radius not invited. Their son, Brett, and I were pretty good friends, but for some reason his mom and dad didn't want me at the party.

I'll never forget that day. With no fence separating our backyards I watched what turned out to be one of the coolest parties our neighborhood ever threw. I cried some pretty heavy 10-year-old tears that day as I experienced my very first case of feeling rejected.

Ouch! My Heart

To this day I doubt you could make a convincing case that there is any feeling more painful than that of *not* being included—the feeling of rejection. It's a horrible feeling because of what being rejected makes us wonder about ourselves. Somehow we fall short of somebody's ideal, making us not good enough for whatever we want to be a part of.

To some extent we've all felt it, haven't we? Whether it's someone telling you they've fallen out of love with you or an employer telling you they no longer need your services, the sting of rejection is real pain and doesn't heal quickly.

I think the hardest I ever felt that pain was when I was 19 years old. I'd met a girl named Ruth in a fast-food restaurant where we both worked. One day I mustered up the courage to ask her out. After the date she gave me a little kiss and went into the house, leaving me to drive home with a smile on my face and hope in my heart.

Over the next few months Ruth and I were together nearly every day. I started saving my money because I had an idea. As summer approached I'd saved enough to pay for Ruth and me to take a vacation together. When I approached her about it, she was excited and asked me what our options were. I said that I'd saved enough for us to go either to Hawaii, Disneyland, or Reno. She thought about it and said, "Can we go to South Dakota?"

"Why would anyone want to go to South Dakota—on purpose?" I asked. She explained that she'd lived there for a couple of years and still had some friends and family there that she wanted me to meet.

I agreed. About a month later we packed up and drove my truck to South Dakota. It was really neat for us to drive and talk together. The trip seemed to be drawing us closer and closer. At last we pulled into the little town of Huron, South Dakota. We unloaded our things and settled into the house of some friends of her parents. We had dinner with them and were having a nice visit in the living room when I heard a knock on their front door.

Ruth answered the door and brought a young man about her age into the living room with her. She introduced him to me as "Keith, my ex-boyfriend." My unbiased opinion was that he was short and ugly. After a few minutes of conversation, Keith turned and asked if he and Ruth could walk around the block together, "just to say hi."

What could I say? They left, and there I sat all by myself with people I'd met just two hours before. We waited. We small-talked. We waited. When Ruth finally got back, she informed me that I was no longer her boyfriend. She and short ugly Keith were getting back together. As gracefully as I could I cried, got on my knees, and begged her to take me back.

I cooled my heels there in Huron, South Dakota, for a week. At the end of the week I loaded up a bunch of stuff Ruth needed to haul back to Washington State and watched as she mauled, I mean kissed, this guy goodbye. All the way home I begged her to reconsider. With the strength of Wonder Woman she resisted my advances.

When we finally got home we unloaded her stuff, and I drove off. I didn't want to go to my little apartment, so I drove to my mom's house, ran through the front door, raced frantically to my old bedroom, and sobbed on my old bed. My mom sat and ran her fingers through my hair as I cried my pain to her.

It took three months and a really pretty girl to finally get me over the pain of being rejected by a girl I'd really cared about. Do you know the feeling I'm talking about? The feeling of not being included. I couldn't figure out why I didn't measure up. What was wrong with me? I truly just wanted to curl up and die.

Dishing It Out

Now that I'm older, and a little more observant, I've come to realize that not only had I experienced feelings of rejection, but I had also been the source of dishing them out.

When I was in boarding academy I had a girlfriend named Deana. She and I had gone out for about three months when I started to feel ready to move on to another relationship. Unfortunately, I didn't know how or when to tell her. I must have begun acting a little strange, because she noticed that I was different.

One evening as we were riding in the school bus with a bunch of other students to a Valentine's banquet, Deana asked me what was wrong. This was the wrong time to tell her, so I said, "Nothing." After all, we were on the way to a banquet, and it was supposed to be a romantic evening. She kept prying. At last, under great duress, I blurted it out: "I don't think we should see each other anymore."

She cried for days. I became the heel that broke a girl's heart during the Valentine's banquet. For weeks every time I saw her in the hallway she would burst into tears and run into the girls' restroom.

Jesus Felt It Too

Whether it's a breakup with a high school girlfriend, a family member going through a divorce, or a grade school kid whom nobody wants to pick for their team, not being included—rejection—is a brutal reminder to the person it visits that somehow they just don't measure up. It's painful.

Jesus felt rejection. The Bible teaches us that He came to earth with good news about God. He was excited about loving and sharing with the very people He had a hand in creating. What He got was *full-scale rejection.* In fact, the prophet Isaiah calls Him "despised and rejected" (Isaiah 53:3).

The Bible tells us that the very people Christ came to love, beat Him up and nailed Him to a cross. And the rejection He felt was so deep that He felt rejected by God Himself. In agony He cried out, "My God, my God, why have you forsaken me?" (Matthew 27:46, NIV).

Jesus knows what it feels like to be rejected. He knows what it's like to not be included. I think that's why it gives Him so much pleasure to offer you and me the knowledge of a very special gift.

Find a Bible and open it to Ephesians 1. Read the whole chapter, but concentrate on the message of these specific words: "For he chose us in him before the creation of the world to be holy and blameless in his sight. In love he predestined us to be adopted as his sons through Jesus Christ" (Ephesians 1:4, 5, NIV).

In other words, in God's world, before you were even born, God adopted you into His family. Even if until now you haven't given God the time of day, He has accepted you into His family. It's an open invitation with no strings attached. *You are in if you wanna be.* You are accepted by God, chosen by Him, guaranteed.

I work with teenagers a lot. I can't tell you how many times I've heard young people say, "God can't include me; He can't accept me. You don't know what I've done."

Hey, based on what the Bible tells me about God, I don't care what you've done, God's acceptance of you is unconditional. He offers it to you right now. God included you in His kingdom before you were even born. His acceptance is yours for the taking.

So consider yourself included, chosen by God. And the best news about being chosen by God is that He's not going to change His mind about including you in His family. There is no certificate of divorce. He won't hand you a pink slip for doing a bad job at whatever He's called you to do. In the New Testament book of Hebrews God says, "I will never leave you nor forsake you" (Hebrews 13:5, NKJV). He's the best lover, the best boss, the most loyal friend you could ever have.

God has chosen you. Have you chosen Him? You will never find a more faithful, unconditionally accepting life companion.

What the Bible Says About Being Chosen

I have found four principles in the Bible that tell me what it means to be chosen. I've always been a fan of the game show *Jeopardy*. So in the tradition of *Jeopardy* I'll share my four principles as questions.

1. Who chose you? The Bible says that God chose you (Ephesians 1). Not only did He choose you, but Psalm 139:13 says that He actually wove you together in your mother's womb, creating you with all of the uniqueness and specialness that is you.

You've got to love a religion that teaches that God seeks out and chooses His people. He found us long before we ever found Him. In John 15:16 we read that He chose us; we didn't choose Him. Our part in the deal is to just acknowledge that we are chosen and acknowledge the chooser (John 3:16).

2. When were you chosen? The Bible says that you were chosen before the creation of the world (Ephesians 1; Psalm 139). Long before we were even a gleam in our daddy's eye, God thought of us, planned for us, and was excited to receive us into His world.

3. Why were you chosen? The Bible suggests that you were chosen to fit into God's plan for the world in which you live. More specifically, Ephesians 2:10 says, "For we are what he has made us, created in Christ Jesus for good works, which God prepared beforehand to be our way of life" (NRSV). As we will see later in this book, the "good works" that we were created for have a lot to do with how we treat the people around us.

If you want to get a better notion of what God chooses people for, read the story of Joseph in the book of Genesis. There is a crucial point in the story where Joseph's brothers discover who he is. They become filled with fear, because years earlier they'd treated him shamefully, beat him up, thrown him into a pit, and finally sold him into slavery. Joseph, realizing what it meant to be chosen, responded with words that must have made God smile. Genesis 45 records his response: "And now do not be distressed, or angry with yourselves, because you sold me here; *for God sent me before you to preserve life. . . So it was not you who sent me here, but God;* he has made me a father to Pharaoh, and lord of all his house and ruler over all the land of Egypt" (verses 5-8, NRSV).

Joseph could have been bitter about his life, but he wasn't. He knew God had a plan for his life, and that he had been chosen to play out that plan.

Who knows what God's plan is for your life? I know that sometimes it seems the plan isn't working out like it ought to. But if you trust in God, you will trust in His plan for you, too.

4. Who gets chosen? Lest you start thinking a little too much of yourself, being chosen is not exclusive to any one person or group of people. You've done nothing that's made God like you more than the fellow down the street. In fact, God didn't choose you for any other reason than this: He created you and He loves you. Period. You don't have to be a member of the right church, have the right family heritage, or be better behaved than your neighbor. In fact, the Bible is very clear on God's feelings about who gets chosen. Read some of the texts below to discover whom God wants to call His chosen.

The Lord is not slow about his promise as some count slowness, but is forbearing toward you, *not wishing that any should perish, but that all should reach repentance* (2 Peter 3:9, RSV).

In explaining whom Christ died for on the cross (whom God chose) Paul says this: "Then as one man's trespass led to condemnation for *all men,* so one man's act of righteousness leads to acquittal and life for *all men"* (Romans 5:18, RSV).

First Timothy 2:3, 4 says, "This is good, and it is acceptable in the sight of God our Savior, who desires *all men* to be saved and to come to the knowledge of the truth" (RSV).

First Timothy 4:10 tells us, "For to this end we toil and strive, because we have our hope set on the living God, who is the Savior of *all men,* especially of those who believe" (RSV).

Reading these texts, it's easy to see that the Bible teaches that God has chosen all people to be saved and all people to be in relationship with Him.

Of course, not everyone wants to be chosen. Many, maybe even most, reject the notion of being God's son or daughter and prefer to go it on their own. Even so, they have been chosen. Christ died for *all* (Titus 2:11), not just the ones who acknowledge Him.

He didn't ask our permission. He didn't consult us. He just created us and chose us as His sons and daughters. And though He has a plan for every chosen person, He has left acknowledging and following our choosing up to us. In other words, we get to choose what we want to do with this information—whether we want to accept our election or not.

Regardless, the good news is, if you are breathing, you are chosen.

CHAPTER 5

PLAYING THE FOOL

Have you ever done something stupid to impress a person of the opposite sex? Now, don't tell me that you haven't. Even in church I see men do it all the time, and you have too. It's the "I'm not that old and out of shape" pose. It kind of goes like this: An attractive younger woman walks by a bunch of middle-aged men. As she walks by, they suck in their guts so hard that half of them rupture a spleen, exhaling quickly when she rounds the corner. Don't worry; everybody does it. It's part of being a middle-aged male.

When I was a teenager, a girl in my neighborhood named Karen captured my attention. One night we were at a friend's house with 15 or so other young people when I noticed that my friend Tim and Karen were making eyes at each other. Not knowing what else to do, I decided to divert attention and impress Karen with my strength. A pull-up bar had been placed between one of the doorjambs close to where Karen and Tim were sitting. I did some pull-ups with the ease of Arnold Schwarzenegger, but that didn't seem to catch Karen's attention, so I started to swing on the bar. Wildly at first, and then more vigorously, until my feet were hitting the ceiling on both ends of my stretch. This amazing feat captured the attention of all in the room, including Karen.

Everything was going along fine until at the top of one of my swings as my body was stretched out parallel to the ground, the bar came loose. My head, always being the heaviest part of my body, came swinging down as my feet shot up. The cement floor and my head met violently with a deadening thud.

When I woke up, I heard laughter. Karen helped me up and offered to walk me down the street to my home. One hundred yards into our journey my stomach decided that I didn't need all the ice cream I'd eaten an hour before.

As I was doubled over losing my lunch, Karen assured me that falling from that pull-up bar was one of the funniest things she'd ever witnessed. To this day, when I go home to Seattle and see my neighborhood friends, somebody usually pops up with "Hey, Witas, remember that time you were showing off and you smashed your head on the cement?" Which is usually followed by some unkind statement like "I guess that explains why he turned out the way he did. Ha, ha, ha."

It seems as though it's just human nature to feel less than adequate from time to time, which produces the need to show off or act like fools. The people or the circumstances around us become intimidating or challenging enough to make us feel we must be more than who we are to be loved or accepted.

From a pretty young age the television programs we watch teach us that happy, loved, successful people look, dress, and act a certain way. We learn that if you aren't naturally one of the beautiful people, you're inadequate and need to somehow make up for your deficiencies.

And when those feelings of inadequacy are at their worst, we don't stop at just showing off. *Many times we put the people around us down in order to make ourselves look all the better.* I became really good at this as a teenager.

Cold Shoulders and Light Erasers

My first day in boarding academy was frightening. It was registration day. The halls were full of students, signing up for their classes and visiting. I'm tall, and when I'm standing in a crowd of strangers it feels to me that I stick out like a sore thumb. I was in desperate need of a familiar face when from the other end of the hallway I heard someone yell my name.

When I looked I saw Scott, a friend of mine from summer camp. I hadn't seen him in four years, but still, he was a friendly face. I think he was hunting a familiar face too, for we made our way through the crowd until we met, and then caught up on old times. We were cruising the hallways talking when we came upon three girls. Scott knew two of them. My first day was going better than I could have imagined. I found someone I knew, and I got to talk to girls.

Soon a bell rang, and people started clearing out of the building. The girls informed us that it was time for lunch. A couple minutes later the hallways were empty. Instead of heading to the cafeteria and standing in long lunch lines, we decided to stay and talk for a while. We were talking and laughing when I heard a rhythmic sound that seemed to be getting closer and closer to where we were standing. Finally I turned around, and I saw a guy speed-walking right for our group.

His hair was slicked back tightly to his head, with a stray strand that bounced as he walked. His black-rimmed glasses were thick with one of the arms held together by a paper clip. His pants were *way* out of style and pulled halfway up his stomach. His shirt was buttoned all the way to the top, and half of his collar stuck up, while the other lay flat. That kid was the quintessential nerd. There was no other way to describe him.

Without slowing down, he burst through the middle of our group and blasted out the doors. It was as if he didn't even see us. I looked at the girls and said, "What was that?"

"Fred!" they said, laughing. Fred was, by their description, the weirdest kid in school. They described all kinds of strange things they'd seen him do (half of them were probably just rumors that achieved academy legend status), and said that it was best just to stay away from him.

By then enough time had passed that the cafeteria lines should be more manageable, so we decided to head out the door for lunch.

As we left the building we saw a large green trash receptacle to our right. To my amazement and amusement, standing in the middle of the trash reading a newspaper was Fred. I'd never seen anything like it. He stood there in the trash, reading, just as if he were a businessman reading the *Wall Street Journal* while waiting in an airport to catch a plane.

The girls and I again started laughing. They called him a couple of names, making sure he heard them. He just ignored us and kept reading.

When we got to the cafeteria, we found that there was a girls' line and a guys' line (that's how they did things in the olden days). When you went through line to get your food, you didn't just sit where you wanted to. You had to sit at the table where the student hosts were standing. Three guys and three girls were assigned to a table, seated as they came out of their respective food lines. Scott and I waited until we saw the three girls we'd come in with, then rushed out so that we were seated with them. This left one empty seat.

You guessed it. About five minutes later the host seated Fred at our table. As soon as he sat down, we turned and gave him the cold shoulder. We made it plain that whatever conversation we were engaged in, he was not to enter. We actually forgot that he was even there until he started choking on some food. With a cataclysmic blast, Fred coughed up whatever was blocking his airways, spraying a combination of chewed-up beans and cheese all over our trays and plates. The girls wheeled around and started screaming at him in disgust. Finally I got the last word in. "Fred, you idiot, why don't you just get out of here!" Flustered by all of the unexpected attention, he quickly gathered up his tray and ushered himself out of the cafeteria.

For the next year, if Fred happened to walk toward me on one side of the hallway I went to the other side. If he was the only person in a room I had to enter, most of the time I'd wait until someone else went in first. It wasn't that I didn't like him; I didn't even know him. I do know that even though we were both students on a small academy campus, I didn't speak to him all year.

And then one day about a month before graduation, I was in the ad building late, looking for some books that I'd left there. (If you had looked at my GPA, you would have known they were not school books.) As I walked down the hallway I saw a light on in the history room. I peeked in and saw Fred, standing in the middle of a bunch of empty desks. He held a pencil in his hand, eraser out. He was moving the pencil around in the air as if he were directing a choir.

I kept peeking through the door, trying to figure out what on earth he was doing. And then my curiosity got the best of me. I entered the room, sat down at one of the desks, and said, "Hey, Fred, what are you doing?"

He didn't even look at me when he answered, "Inventing."

"Inventing what?"

"I'm inventing a light eraser," he said. He pointed to the end of the pencil and explained, "I'm going to invent an object that can erase localized light. I'm going to make it so that I can stand in a lighted room and erase the light in the middle of it without using shadows."

It actually sounded like a cool idea, although I had no idea what someone would use it for. Then Fred stopped what he was doing, looked at me, and said, "Why are you talking to me?"

He caught me off guard. I didn't really know what to say. "What do you mean?" I stammered. "I talk to you."

"No, you don't. The only words you've ever said to me were when you called me an idiot and told me to leave the cafeteria." He didn't seem to be sad or angry about it, just matter-of-fact.

"Well, I'm talking to you now, aren't I? How's it going?" Fred and I talked for what seemed like a couple of hours. He told me things about his family life that I couldn't believe. I thought *I* had a challenging life. As we talked I began to understand who Fred was and why he'd become the "odd" person he seemed to be. I really felt sorry for the guy. I also found out that he wasn't an idiot after all (he got better grades than I did!).

That afternoon I met with some of my friends and asked them to do me a favor. I asked them if they'd treat Fred like one of the guys for the last couple weeks of school. They agreed, and for the next two weeks every time we saw him in the hallway we said, "Hi" and made him feel that he was a friend. I guess it was probably the first time in his life that he'd even been noticed, not to mention treated as a friend.

I guess our kindness toward Fred caught on because the next year at graduation, when his name was called, the student body cheered and clapped. Fred stopped halfway across the stage and raised both arms, as if to say "I did it! I finally made it."

For a whole year I was willing to put a pretty frail young man, a boy without a hope of friendship with anyone, through hell—just so I could look good to the people around me. Behavior like that really went against my better nature, but I found myself acting like somebody else so that I could fit in with those who were important to me at the time.

Have you ever done this?

Have you let the need to "fit in" change your behavior, or worse yet, dictate who you are as a person? The Bible tells us about a man who got caught doing exactly this. His name was Peter.

Peter and Our Looking Glass

Peter was one of Jesus' best friends, and had been commissioned by Jesus to go out and tell people the good news about how much God loved them. The problem with that—for Peter—was that Peter was a Jew. And in Peter's society, if you were going to be a Jew of any status or importance, you wouldn't be caught dead with the "wrong" kind of people.

Peter was in Antioch one day having a meal with a large group of people from a different culture and sharing the good news of God with them. The people he was talking with were actually starting to understand who Jesus was and how He could affect their lives, when something unexpected happened. The door to the room opened, and some folks from Peter's church—rich and influential folks—walked in. Immediately Peter realized the kind of people he was with. They didn't dress as nice, they didn't act quite the same, and they certainly didn't eat the same things Peter's friends did. Overcome with embarrassment, Peter excused himself from the group he was with and sat with the group that had come through the door. Peter's guests felt the cold shoulder, and Peter's hypocrisy was exposed to all in the room.

Peter's decision to get up and get back with the "in" crowd influenced others to do the same thing. One of Jesus' most ardent followers saw what Peter did and followed his example, making a similar decision to turn his back on his new friends. You can read all about it in Galatians 2.

Why would anyone do such a thing? I believe the reason we sometimes act in strange ways to make ourselves look better or different than we are is that we insist on seeing ourselves in the mirror of *our accomplishments,* the *people we hang around,* and *the things we possess.*

In high school I more or less placed value on myself depending on how many points I scored during a basketball game. If I had a particularly bad game, or lost my cool and ended up getting thrown out, my self-opinion plummeted, and I'd end up blaming the refs or tearing my teammates down in order to build back my self-esteem.

Each of us is tempted in different ways to allow temporal things to determine our self identity. For some of us it's our careers. For others it's our status or economic success. And from day to day our self-esteem can depend on how we look, the clothes we wear, the car we drive, or the attention we receive from the right people in our lives.

The problem that we face, measuring our personal value with such temporary, mundane things, is that they all stand a good chance of passing away. What happens to the self-esteem of the ballplayer who blows a knee and can't play ball anymore? What happens to the wealthy person who loses everything in a bad investment? What happens when everything that you've tied your identity to is no longer a part of your life?

All of our lives, our friends and family, the media, our government, and even our churches have been telling us what we must do in order to fit in. We're either too fat or too skinny. Maybe we don't drive the right car, have a big enough savings account, haven't seen the latest movie, or we don't wear the latest Nikes to come off the line. Maybe we're told that if we don't practice or believe the right things, we don't measure up spiritually. And somewhere in the back of our minds, something or someone is telling us that we aren't good enough. We think that maybe if we can just appear smarter or more educated or acquire a few more nice things we'll be accepted faster and like ourselves more.

And in the midst of all the voices telling us how incomplete we are, a still small voice is straining to tell us something different about ourselves. If we would just listen to this voice, we would know the truth about who we really are.

God's Value System

God's message to you and to me about who we are and what we're made of is best articulated by King David, a man who lived in Old Testament times and had a passion for God. I discovered this passage the night that my birth mother found me, and I think it's worth looking at again. It's in Psalm 139. It says, "O Lord, you have searched me and you know me. . . . You created my inmost being; you knit me together in my mother's womb. I praise you because I am fearfully and wonderfully made; your works are wonderful, I know that full well. My frame was not hidden from you when I was made in the secret place. When I was woven together in the depths of the earth, your eyes saw my unformed body. All the days ordained for me were written in your book before one of them came to be" (verses 1-16, NIV).

In other words, the Bible says this: God is the one who is

responsible for putting you together *just like you are.* You are not some cosmic accident that somehow has to show off or put other people down to make yourself look good. You are fine just the way you are, just as God made you to be. And He loves you. In fact, He loves you so much that the Bible says He would actually rather die than live without you.

Because of this, you have the unequaled status as a son or a daughter of God. You are priceless in the eyes of your Creator. No job, no car, no human influence can add to your status in God's eyes. Because of Jesus' death and resurrection, *God values you more than any entity in the universe.* God has chosen you. And God wants you and me to realize this and start acting like it.

It's when we accept this that we can stop the charade. We no longer have to place our self-esteem in the hands of the scale we are standing on, or in the hands of the people around us. We no longer have to view ourselves through the lens of a career, or the way the media or others would have us evaluate our own value. We don't have to measure ourselves by anybody else's standard anymore.

It's when we internalize how much God loves and values us—*just as we are*—that we can start treating the people around us, no matter who they are or what they look like, with the respect and the dignity they deserve as chosen sons and daughters of God.

It's time to stop letting the world tell us how invaluable we are. It's time to listen to the voice of God and thank Him for the value He put on us when He created us and chose us. It's time to internalize and own the words of Romans 8:39: "Neither height nor depth, nor anything else in all creation, will be able to separate us from the love of God that is in Christ Jesus our Lord" (NIV).

CHAPTER 6

CHOSEN PEOPLE ARE LIGHT REFLECTORS

Walking in the Dark

When I was young, I was afraid of the dark. I'm not sure why I was afraid of the dark; I just was. I think that at one time or another, most kids are. There was a cemetery about 10 city blocks from my childhood home, and one time when some friends and I were sleeping overnight in the tree house we started playing truth or dare. When it was my turn I bravely chose to take a dare. I couldn't believe what my friend Dennis dared me to do. I had to walk through the cemetery by myself, fill a paper cup with some water from the fountain in the middle of the graveyard, and walk back to the front gate, where my friends would all be waiting on their bikes.

I'd walked through that same cemetery lots of times before—in the daylight. In fact, during the daytime hours, I would frequently skateboard the hills, hunt for frogs in the water near the fountains, and walk my motorbike through the cemetery to get to a set of riding trails just behind it.

But walking through it at night . . . this was a different story. I took extra care that I stayed on the cement paths, worried that something might reach up and grab me. There has never been a preteen heart so ready to explode. It was incredibly frightening. Why? *Because I was walking in the dark.* I didn't know what was out there. I was hearing things that I'm sure weren't making any noise. I was afraid because I was walking in the dark.

One of the games that we made up in the little Adventist grade school I attended was called "blind man, blind man." In the game my friends and I would go onto the stage behind the gymnasium stage curtain and set up all kinds of obstacles. Then we'd dub one person as "it," shut off the lights, and try to make it from one end of the stage to the other without being tagged. It was so dark that we couldn't see our hands directly in front of our faces. I remember countless times that we'd hear a loud *thud,* turn on the lights, and see that someone had tripped over an obstacle and smacked their head on a metal chair. Playing in the light would have been a simple game of tag. Playing in the dark added an element of danger that made the game more challenging.

Walking in the Light

The Bible tells us in Ephesians 5 and in 1 John 1 that as God's chosen we are to walk in the light. What exactly does it mean to walk in the light? How does a person who walks in the light act? What do they do and not do? How are they different from a person who walks in the darkness?

When I did a word search on my computer Bible program, the number of times the words "light" and "dark" or "darkness" appeared in the same set of verses showed more than 400 hits. The Bible has a lot to say about what it means to walk in the light.

The first thing I discovered in my study about what it means to walk in the light was the most obvious. When you walk in the light you can clearly see what was once hidden by darkness. It's just like the "blind man, blind man" game we played as children. It was easy to maneuver our way through the obstacles when the light was on, but when we chose to walk in the darkness we fell down and hit our heads a lot.

The spiritual implications of walking in the light versus walking in the darkness are the same. John 11:9, 10 says this: "Jesus answered, 'Are there not twelve hours of daylight? Those who walk during the day do not stumble, because they see the light of this world. But those who walk at night stumble, because the light is not in them'" (NRSV).

When we choose to walk in the light, we can more clearly make our way through the obstacles that Satan has set in our path. Walking in the light makes many of these obstacles plain, helping us to identify where and what they are. In other words, we come to the point where we clearly know the difference between good and evil and can see to avoid the evil. Walking in the light helps us to avoid obstacles that can critically damage us spiritually or even kill us physically.

Walking in the darkness doesn't afford us the opportunity to avoid the traps and snares that the evil one has set in our life paths. If we choose to walk in the darkness (rejecting that God has chosen us for good), feeling our way down the course of our lives, it's inevitable that something will trip us up, something we didn't see coming. Walking in the dark changes our ideas of what is right and wrong to the point where our value system ends up with "no light in it at all."

What we used to think was wrong behavior becomes not only tolerable, it actually becomes right, or at least morally neutral. We catch ourselves saying things such as, "Well, there's nothing really wrong with it." Matthew 6:23 records that Jesus put it this way: "If your eye is unhealthy, your whole body will be full of darkness. If then the light in you is darkness, how great is the darkness!" (NRSV).

In other words, some folks can walk in the darkness for so long that the light that they used to have is tainted by darkness.

Walking in the light not only allows us to see the traps and snares of the evil one; it also allows us to walk confidently. Cemeteries aren't scary places in the daytime. Walking in the light carries with it boldness and assurance. That's why the author of Psalm 23 could boldly say, "Yea, though I walk through the valley of the shadow of death, I will fear no evil; for thou art with me" (verse 4).

Walking in the light helps us to see life and its challenges more clearly, and to walk through life with assurance and confidence.

If we walk in the light, we can walk confidently, without fear.

Light Equals Truth

The second thing I discovered about walking in the light is that it is synonymous with walking in the truth. Isaiah 8:20 tells us, "To the law and to the testimony! If they do not speak according to this word, *it is* because *there is no light* in them" (NKJV).

In other words, if whatever you are saying or hearing is not truth, then it either is darkness or comes from the darkness.

People who walk in the light are people who are interested in the truth. Now, we have to be careful what we do with this verse. Is there anyone on the earth who has full knowledge of all truth? No. The only person in the universe who has knowledge of absolute truth is God Himself.

Unfortunately, we have used this *law and testimony* verse in arrogant ways. Once when I had invited a non-Adventist pastor to speak at my church an angry church member stormed into my office to protest. I asked what the problem was, and she said, "He doesn't keep the Sabbath, so there is no light in him!"

I was dumbfounded. I didn't even have a response. Then this dear woman opened up the Bible and pointed to this verse in Isaiah, saying, "If they don't speak from the law and to the testimony, there is no light in them!"

I'm not sure if it was divine inspiration that led me to my response, but I suddenly thought of what Ellen White said about Martin Luther, one of the great Reformers. I quickly found some of those things on a CD-ROM and showed her. She looked at me and said, "So what's your point?" Then I went to my library and showed her some translated writings of what Martin Luther had to say about the Sabbath. He didn't like Jews or their Sabbath, and he didn't have very nice things to say about them either. The woman let me have our non-Adventist guest come in and speak.

Read in context, what this verse in Isaiah says is simply this:

"Don't seek light from darkness. Don't try to twist evil things to make them look good. Don't make excuses. Just live by the truth that God has given in His Word, and leave it at that."

The verse is actually addressing a problem that Israel had with going to wizards and spiritual mediums to seek out answers for their problems. They were seeking to live a life that was popular in their culture, but against God's expressed wishes for them. In contemporary terms, Isaiah is saying, *"Live your life according to the standards that God has given you and not by the pressures and dictates of your culture."*

To Have and to Hold, if It Feels Right

Walking outside of the truth is becoming more and more popular today, isn't it? Now, I'm not necessarily talking about people having the wrong theology. I'm talking more specifically about God's chosen people who know the truth but choose to act on their feelings instead.

Sometimes when I'm driving in the morning I'll turn on the radio and listen to a program hosted by a woman known as Dr. Laura. I like listening to talk radio, whether I always agree with the host or not. One day a young woman called in to Dr. Laura for advice. She said that she'd been seeing a guy for some time and that she was now living with him. She felt as though they should get married.

What complicated the matter was that she'd started seeing him while he was still married. He had divorced his wife and moved in with this girl, but didn't seem to want to marry her. When Dr. Laura asked why she would date a married man in the first place, the girl responded by saying, "It just *feels* like we are meant to be together. It *feels* like we are meant for each other."

Dr. Laura went off on this poor girl. "Since when are your feelings the basis for the major decisions that you make in your life?" she asked.

The girl responded, "Well, what else am I supposed to go on?"

I was glad for Dr. Laura's answer. She said, "How about the Ten

Commandments?" She went on to explain that today's society is plagued with divorce, adultery, and misbehavior by children and adults because we have replaced values (truth or light) with feelings.

I can't tell you how many of my divorced friends told me that "our *feelings* just changed for each other." What does that have to do with anything? When you stood at the altar and made promises to God and to your bride, did you say, "I promise to love, honor, and cherish you until death do us part—or until my feelings change for you"?

The promise I made at the altar had nothing to do with my feelings, it had to do with my commitment. My marriage better not have its roots established in my feelings. Feelings change from week to week and year to year. My marriage better be established in my commitment. That commitment is a promise to love my wife until the day death takes one of us away.

How many times have we let our feelings replace what we know is truth? Have you ever let your feelings—instead of truth—dictate your choice of entertainment? the food you eat? the language you use? the way you treat the people around you?

I can't tell you how many times I've heard someone say, "I couldn't help my behavior because I was feeling . . ."

People who walk in the light walk in the truth. They let the truth dictate their actions and make decisions for them, not their feelings or emotions. Do you think Jesus *felt* like going to the cross? I'm glad that Jesus decided to walk in the light, because if He had made His Gethsemane decision on feelings alone things would be much different than they are.

People who walk in the light walk in the truth.

City on a Hill

The third thing I discovered about walking in the light is that those who walk in the light also reflect the light. In Matthew 5 Jesus calls His chosen ones the "light of the world." Isaiah 58:10 tells us that "if you offer your food to the hungry and satisfy the needs of the afflicted, then your light shall rise in the darkness and your gloom be like the noonday" (NRSV).

Reflecting the light of God in our life isn't necessarily something we strive for, *it's who we become* as we walk in the light. Psalm 112:1-4 says, "Praise the Lord! Happy are those who fear the Lord, who greatly delight in his commandments. Their descendants will be mighty in the land; the generation of the upright will be blessed. Wealth and riches are in their houses, and their righteousness endures forever. They rise in the darkness as a light for the upright; they are gracious, merciful, and righteous" (NRSV).

Jesus didn't say, "You *should* become the light of the world." He said, "You *are* the light of the world. He said, "You can't hide it; it's like a city on a hill. It just happens."

When we are walking in the light, as He is in the light, that light will attract people out of the darkness just as surely as a porch light can draw a moth to it from a long distance away.

Perhaps you've experienced it. Friends or associates who felt the urge to bring up your spiritual life. Something in the way you walk in the light compelled them to bring it up in a conversation, or maybe in a note of thanks. One of the most beautiful things about being a light reflector is the effect you can have on the people around you. God's chosen people, those who choose to walk in the light, are truly reflectors of Christ's character. Not perfect representations, but certainly reflectors of the light of Christ, and not of darkness.

Lovers of the Light Love to Love

The last thing that I've discovered about walking in the light is that people who do so have an overabundant capacity to love. Their decision to love people is an extension of their love for Christ.

The Bible says it this way in 1 John 2:9, 10: "Whoever says, 'I am in the light,' while hating a brother or sister, is still in the darkness.

Whoever loves a brother or sister lives in the light, and in such a person there is no cause for stumbling" (NRSV).

Do you want to know if you're walking in the light? Do a heart check. How do you feel about those you share your life with, people whom you agree with and disagree with? How do you feel about the children of God whom you come into contact with every day? How do you treat people?

Is your need to be self-important or to get a laugh more important than the person who is the object of your joke? Do you enjoy tearing people down when they aren't there to defend themselves? Do you find yourself being more concerned with your personal comfort than with the well-being of others? Do you find yourself so concerned about being right theologically that you're willing to alienate the people who disagree with you?

A friend of mine has entered into a period of questioning her faith. In her questioning, she has gotten extremely skeptical and critical of what her church believes and has established as its doctrine. Now, questioning, and even adjusting your beliefs according to God's leading in your life, is healthy. I believe that. Unfortunately, what's happened in this case is that she is so convinced she's right that she barely allows friends and family to have their own beliefs. If they don't agree with her, she considers them "closed-minded" and "incapable of thinking out of the box."

This is kind of God's gut check. Are you walking in the light, as He is in the light? Has your capacity to love and have compassion lessened in time or has it grown? Has your passion for the well-being of people who walk in the darkness been growing or shrinking as you've grown in your knowledge of the truth?

Now, don't get it backward. Don't try to do all of these things so that you can walk in the light. Walk in the light, and, by God's grace, you will become all of these things.

And how do you walk in the light? You know the answer to that. John 8:12 tells us that Jesus said, "I am the light of the world.

Whoever follows me will never walk in darkness, but will have the light of life" (NIV).

Walking in the light is making the inconvenient decision to walk as Jesus did. As the book of Revelation puts it, it's "following the Lamb wherever He goes." It's turning your back on a world that has nothing but darkness to offer, and choosing to walk the difficult narrow path—the path of light. It's the life of the chosen of God.

CHAPTER 7

AFRAID OF THE MASTER

Matthew 25 records a parable that hits at the heart of why chosen people don't act chosen. They suffer from a simple emotion that affects all of us at one time or another, and can be debilitating. However, when we face and walk through it, this emotion becomes of no consequence to the great things that God has called us to do.

"Again, it will be like a man going on a journey, who called his servants and entrusted his property to them. To one he gave five talents of money, to another two talents, and to another one talent, each according to his ability. Then he went on his journey. The man who had received the five talents went at once and put his money to work and gained five more. So also, the one with the two talents gained two more. But the man who had received the one talent went off, dug a hole in the ground and hid his master's money. After a long time the master of those servants returned and settled accounts with them. The man who had received the five talents brought the other five. 'Master,' he said, 'you entrusted me with five talents. See, I have gained five more.'

"His master replied, 'Well done, good and faithful servant! You have been faithful with a few things; I will put you in charge of many things. Come and share your master's happiness!'

"The man with the two talents also came. 'Master,' he said, 'you entrusted me with two talents; see, I have gained two more.'

"His master replied, 'Well done, good and faithful servant! You have been faithful with a few things; I will put you in charge of many things. Come and share your master's happiness!'

"Then the man who had received the one talent came. 'Master,' he said, 'I knew that you are a hard man, harvesting where you have not sown and gathering where you have not scattered seed. So I was afraid and went out and hid your talent in the ground. See, here is what belongs to you' " (verses 14-25, NIV).

If the master in this parable represents our Father in heaven, how would you expect Him to reply? Maybe you'd expect something like "Boy, I surely wish you'd have done something with the talent I gave you. Well, at least you didn't lose everything. Better safe than sorry, I guess. Let's hug, and next time do a little better, OK?"

But that's not the response of the Master at all. Keep reading.

"His master replied, 'You wicked, lazy servant! So you knew that I harvest where I have not sown and gather where I have not scattered seed? Well then, you should have put my money on deposit with the bankers, so that when I returned I would have received it back with interest. Take the talent from him and give it to the one who has the ten talents. For everyone who has will be given more, and he will have an abundance. Whoever does not have, even what he has will be taken from him. And throw that worthless servant outside, into the darkness, where there will be weeping and gnashing of teeth' " (verses 26-30, NIV).

I've got a question for you. What was the root of the lazy servant's problem? What made him bury the talent he was given? Look back at verse 25: "I was afraid" (NIV).

Think back to times you were truly afraid. I'm not talking about the kind of fear that happens when you walk around a corner and someone jumps out and yells, "Boo!" That's called getting startled.

I'm talking about the kind of fear that paralyzes you to the point that you alter your intentions. Maybe you really wanted to try a new activity, or join in on something, but you were so afraid you took a pass and were left wondering what you'd missed. I'm not talking about a clinical phobia here. Just plain old fear.

What are you afraid of? Has that fear prevented you from doing something that you've either wanted to do, been called to do, or more importantly, been chosen to do?

I have a couple of fears. One, which I have never been able to conquer, is the fear of singing in front of people. I can sing in a group. I can lead out in a song service. Just don't ask me to sing a solo in front of people. I remember the first time I ever had to do it. It was awful.

I entered boarding academy life when I was in grade 11. As I looked at the options in my schedule, I discovered that I could get out of taking Spanish if I joined the choir. I knew how to read music, and I could sing a little, so I figured I was a lock to make the choir.

Well, I discovered that you didn't need to have that much talent to join the choir. In fact, there were nearly 100 members. I'll never forget two things that happened on my first day of choir. First, the girl sitting in front of me was named Jan. She was pretty, and I wanted to get better acquainted. Second, Mrs. Jorgenson, our director, announced, "This choir will do limited touring. The official touring choir will be selected from this group as you audition for the Sylvan Choir."

Sylvan Choir was composed of 25 students who would tour our constituency and, this particular year, sing at Disneyland and Knott's Berry Farm. I didn't care about Disney or Knott's Berry Farm but I developed a burning desire to audition when I discovered that Jan was a lock for Sylvan Choir. So I decided to try out.

I tried out. I made the cut, and to my great surprise, I got to stand close to Jan during every rehearsal. Life was good—until Mrs. Jorgenson handed out the syllabus for the class. In order to stay in Sylvan and pass the class, each member had to sing two solos—one sacred, one secular.

My palms sweat even now just thinking about it. I had to make a choice. Let my fear take me out of the "Jan sweepstakes," or face my fear and sing the song. I decided to face my fear. I practiced my song every day in the practice rooms. I got to where—in the practice room—I wasn't afraid at all. It was sort of like singing in the shower.

But then my time of truth arrived: October of 1978, in the Mossyrock, Washington, Seventh-day Adventist Church. There were probably only 50 people there. I didn't know any of them. The scripture was read, the prayer was said, the offering was taken. It was time for special music.

And, as it turned out, it was quite special. I got up, sang, and finished. After I finished, I heard the obligatory "Amen" from an old man in the back of the room.

After church I asked my director, "So, what did you think? Did it sound OK?"

She was a very *direct* director. "You sounded fine," she said, "but you looked like a moron!"

It turns out that while I was singing I nervously grabbed the sides of my pants, which hiked them up above my sock line. Feet spread apart, I rocked back and forth during the whole song. She said that my face "looked like a deer in headlights."

All the way back to the school, my fellow choir members tried to encourage me, saying such things as, "You know, it didn't look that bad. . . . OK, well, yes, it did! You really looked funny! Ha, ha, ha."

You know what? All of their laughing and good-natured jabbing didn't really matter much to me on that day. No matter what they said, I knew that I'd done it. I'd sung the song.

There's nothing like the feeling of walking through your fear. You know what else? There's nothing like the defeated feeling you get when you let your fears make you walk away.

Just recently I saw the look of victory associated only with walking through a fear. I watched some of the seniors and their sponsors in the academy where I pastor, during a program we call Senior Survival. You should have seen it as our girls' dean, Mrs. Wright, stood above us, back turned, arms crossed, and plunged backward into our waiting arms. It's called the *trust fall.*

At the beginning of the week Dean Wright had told me that she'd help out in any way possible—except doing the trust fall. She was terrified. Now, mind you, this is a woman who has survived cancer and cancer treatments. She's raised two daughters (and is still raising a husband). On top of that, she lives in a dorm with 45 teenage girls every school year. You'd think that a woman who has been through so much wouldn't have a fear in the world. But she did. Falling. She didn't like the feeling of falling, especially falling backward.

But there she stood, watching student after student exhibit their trust in their fellow classmates. Even 300-pound student, Bob, took the plunge. Finally, after every classmate and every sponsor fell backward into our waiting arms, Mrs. Wright made her way up on the stage. You could see her fear. She was trembling. The students started chanting her name. And she did it! She walked through her fear, and she became a better person for it. Not only was it good for Dean Wright, but seeing her do it encouraged everyone around her. The fact that she was willing to contribute to the cause of building trust and community within the senior class and the staff at Mount Pisgah Academy did wonders for the morale of the whole program.

What's your fear? How can you walk through it?

The Bible records numerous cases of fear, and only God knows how earth history would have changed if fear had not been the deciding factor in those cases.

~ Fear kept all the disciples except Peter in the boat the night Christ walked across the water to join them. What would have happened to the faith walk of those 11 boat squatters if they had had the faith to walk through their fear and run out to the open arms of a beckoning Master? What would that have done for the Master? It didn't happen, though, did it? They let their fear keep them in the boat, and Peter was the only friend of Jesus to grow that night.

~ Year after year fear kept the Israelites grumbling in the

wilderness. What would have happened if they had walked through their fear, trusted in the God of the fiery pillar, and faced their enemies with God's blessings? Maybe they would have spent 40 years less in the wilderness. Maybe they would have been a nation of evangelists instead of a nation of soldiers. Maybe Zion could have been that city on a hill that God wanted for them all along. Fear kept Israel from becoming what God wanted them to become.

~ It was fear that hid Adam and Eve in the forest away from a loving Savior. What would have happened that cool evening if Adam and Eve had run to their Creator and Savior when they heard His call? What would that have done for the heart of God? Can you imagine how it made God feel to know that His children were afraid of Him? What a tragedy. Fortunately, we have a lot of examples where fear did not rule the day.

~ It was fear that gripped Moses in front of that burning bush, calling him, trying to woo him away from greatness. But Moses didn't let it happen. He knew that he'd been chosen for a special purpose. He walked through his fear. And by doing so he left a legacy of servant leadership that has gone down in history. He truly conquered his fear to do great things for God.

~ Fear must have shaken the prostitute Mary to the core at the doorway in Simon's house, alabaster box in hand, peering into a room full of men who had used her services many times before. But Mary didn't let that fear rip away her opportunity to do something great for her God and her friend. She walked right through that fear, knelt at Jesus' feet, and performed one of the most beautiful acts of sacrifice and love found in Scripture (Matthew 26).

THE GOLDEN HANDCUFFS

Ponder this powerful text about fear and overcoming.

"For God hath not given us the spirit of fear; but of power, and of love, and of a sound mind" (2 Timothy 1:7).

God hasn't given us a spirit of fear. Can you honestly say that you've lived your life with boldness? Can you say that when you've sensed your call to walk on water, or to lead your people, or face that fiery furnace you didn't let fear squelch the great things God has called you to do?

One of the greatest contributors to fear is what my dad used to call "the golden handcuffs." He told me when I was young, "Do all the things that you want to do right now. Don't wait until you are older. When you get older you will have a family and bills and responsibilities. You will have money saved and money to spend. All that stuff will make it so that you won't do the things you want to do now. You will be disabled by the golden handcuffs."

Golden handcuffs are what held the rich young ruler back from doing great things for God (Matthew 19). He was chosen. He knew it, but he couldn't get free of those golden handcuffs.

Matt. 19:16-24 tells of a man who came to Jesus and asked, " 'Teacher, what good thing must I do to get eternal life?'

" 'Why do you ask me about what is good?' Jesus replied. 'There is only One who is good. If you want to enter life, obey the commandments.'

" 'Which ones?' the man inquired.

"Jesus replied, ' "Do not murder, do not commit adultery, do not steal, do not give false testimony, honor your father and mother," and "love your neighbor as yourself." '

" 'All these I have kept,' the young man said. 'What do I still lack?'

"Jesus answered, 'If you want to be perfect, go, sell your possessions and give to the poor, and you will have treasure in heaven. Then come, follow me.'

"When the young man heard this, he went away sad, because he had great wealth.

"Then Jesus said to his disciples, 'I tell you the truth, it is hard for a rich man to enter the kingdom of heaven. Again I tell you, it is easier for a camel to go through the eye of a needle than for a rich man to enter the kingdom of God' " (NIV).

Jesus knew about the golden handcuffs. He knew how they could cause the kind of life comfort that would contribute to the kind of fear that could keep us from doing the very things God has chosen us to do.

Have the golden handcuffs of life been preventing you from doing great things for God? Have they contributed to your fear? Have you been called to give your time, talents, money, or energy to something that you would love to believe in, but have been afraid that the giving of these things would disrupt the comfort of you or your family? Is it possible that you have let fear keep you from the very purpose God has chosen you for?

The Key to the Golden Handcuffs

Two of the people whom I respect more than most in this world are Rob and Renee. I graduated from academy with Rob. Renee was a class behind. They ended up marrying and raising a family after academy. When I knew Rob he wasn't particularly a spiritual guy. In fact, I think I could safely say that he was more apathetic than anything else. He was always a nice guy, just not one whom I would have classed as a person "in tune with God."

I hadn't seen Rob for years. Then one summer as I was preaching at a camp meeting in northwestern Washington, I saw Rob and Renee. I stopped them to catch up with their lives—see what they were doing. I was amazed by the story that they told me.

Somewhere along the line, Rob and Renee had what a good friend of mine calls a *come to Jesus meeting*. They had done pretty well in life—made a good living. Then one day Rob and Renee responded to a call. They decided to sell much of their stuff, put the rest of it in storage, and move their whole family to Mexico and work for an orphanage.

When they told me what they were doing, my response was knee-jerk. "Are you nuts? What about your kids? What about all your stuff? How long are you going to do this?"

Rob just smiled. "We'll stay as long as God can use us down there."

Wow. No fear. Just love and conviction. Wouldn't it be neat to live a life like that? Wouldn't it be neat to give when God moved you to give, without any fear? Wouldn't it be neat to be like Abraham (or Rob) and move when and where God told you to move? Wouldn't it be incredible to live a life free of fear? Rob and Renee found the key to their golden handcuffs—a realization that God had chosen them for a special work. I have a feeling that as long as they are breathing, Rob and Renee will be fear-free, chosen people.

I want that kind of faith. I want to be so wrapped in the love of God that He can say "Jump" and my automatic response will be "How high?"

What's got you afraid? Your past? Your responsibilities? Your self-perception? Whatever it is, could it be holding you back from doing great things for God? I hope not. Because if it is, you don't know what you are missing. Right, Rob?

CHAPTER 8

THE CHANGING CHOSEN

Being a youth pastor in the Seattle area was a comfortable appointment for me because I had grown up in the area and was able to maintain childhood friendships while pastoring a large youth group. None of my old neighborhood buddies were unduly intimidated by the fact that I was now a pastor. In fact, they thought it was kind of cool. They figured that maybe now they had a closer in with God.

Sadly, some of them also allowed me to use their lives as demonstration models for my youth group on how *not* to turn out. One of those people was Tim.

Tim wasn't able to experiment with something and then just move on. Everything he did, he did to excess. As a group of young people growing up together, we made some poor choices in the area of substance abuse and experimentation. As most of us grew up, we decided that we didn't want that kind of long-term addiction, so we quit. Tim was not able to quit. He was married at 18 after getting his girlfriend pregnant. He was addicted to drugs, and at age 28 he was on the verge of losing all of his assets, his family, and eventually his life. (Tim was the friend who owned the limo that picked my birth mother and me up at our first meeting.)

One day Tim's young wife called me and asked for some help. Tim had been gone for a week without contacting the family, and they were getting evicted. She asked if I could come over with a pickup truck and load their stuff and take it to a storage shed. I called a girl in my youth group who was openly experimenting with substance abuse and asked her if she'd come and help. I think you can guess why I wanted her to see this.

She agreed, and we drove downtown to help my friend's family move. When we got there we found all 280 pounds of Tim, home at last, lying on the floor in front of a fan. He was unable to move, and his blood pressure was through the roof. He wouldn't let me call paramedics because he didn't want to have to go through another detox. He couldn't even acknowledge my young friend and me as we stepped over him, moving furniture and boxes. He just lay there, cursing under his breath.

After we got all of their stuff moved, settling Tim's wife and kids in a relative's house, Tim sat down with Allison and me to thank us for helping. While talking with us, he just broke down and started sobbing.

At last he got control of himself and began to explain. "My mom and dad, my brothers and sisters, they all think I'm such a loser. They tell me that I should go out and get a job and become successful, whatever that is. Wit," he said to me, "this is all I know how to do. I can sell drugs and party. This is who I am, and I don't think I can change."

This is who I am, and I don't think I can change. In Tim's case, that was a prophetic statement. A couple of years ago he went over to another neighborhood friend's house, had a needle put in his arm, and drifted away to death.

I got the phone call from his sister the next day. Receiving the news of Tim's death was one of the most heart-wrenching, tragic moments of my life.

This is who I am, and I don't think I can change.

Have you ever thought that? Have you ever thought or said, "This is who I am; this is who God created me to be, so deal with it"?

A lot of people have the idea that between their genetic heritage and their environment, they are who they are, and that's all that they are. People don't change. And to be honest, it kind of seems like that's the truth, doesn't it? In the political arena, whether you think he was a good president or not, most people think that Bill Clinton is who he is. In the sports arena we see numerous athletes who keep falling into drugs, repenting, and then falling into drugs again. The voice of my good friend resonates, *This is who I am, and I don't think I can change.*

But forget about everybody else. Let's just take a look at ourselves. I've thought those thoughts. I've said to myself, "This is who *I* am, and I don't think I can change." At my core, if I'm honest with myself, I am disappointed with who I am. I want to be a great father; I want to be a good husband; I want to be a great chaplain (I want to be a better golfer). But in each case, there are many times when I am less than I want to be.

And then there's the thorns. You know. Everybody's got them. The sins, the character flaws, that just seem to have us handcuffed. The stuff that we just can't shake. The sins that we've asked forgiveness for countless times, promising to never do them again; and then before we know it, we're asking forgiveness for the same sin all over again. Those sins that seem to keep us ever cognizant that we are far from being just like Jesus. *This is who I am, and I don't think I can change.*

Every year I speak with the seniors in my Bible class about expectations. I ask them a pretty direct question: Are the spiritual expectations that you have for yourself and your church being met? And then I give four reasonable expectations that one should have for themselves and for their church:

1. Do you know that you are saved?
2. Does your church's doctrine say incredible things about God?
3. Have you fallen in love with Jesus?
4. Has your character become more and more Christlike through the years?

Of these four, there is one that should be the answer to the self-defeating statement "This is who I am, and I don't think I can change." Chosen people ought to be people who are in a constant mode of change. Look at what the Bible says that God intends for the lives of His chosen people.

"And all of us, with unveiled faces, seeing the glory of the Lord as though reflected in a mirror, are being *transformed* into the same image from one degree of glory to another; for this comes from the Lord, the Spirit" (2 Corinthians 3:18, NRSV).

The words "are being transformed" aren't talking about the possibility of transformed lives; they are talking about the actuality of changing lives.

"Do not be conformed to this world, but be *transformed* by the renewing of your minds, so that you may discern what is the will of God—what is good and acceptable and perfect" (Romans 12:2, NRSV).

"So if anyone is in Christ, there is a new *creation:* everything old has passed away; see, everything has become new!" (2 Corinthians 5:17, NRSV).

"For neither circumcision nor uncircumcision is anything; but a new *creation* is everything!" (Galatians 6:15, NRSV).

A new creation. Transformation. Becoming something that you are not. Like a caterpillar going through rebirth to become a beautiful butterfly.

Being chosen is not supposed to be a static event. Christianity is supposed to be a religion of growth—a religion of transformation, a religion of change. As God's chosen, while retaining the unique personhood that we were created with, spiritually we are to become something we are naturally not.

I did not become a Christian because I was satisfied with who I am. On the contrary, I became a Christian because I saw that who I was, who I am, falls woefully short of who God intends for me to be. And I realized that when I accepted Christ into my life, not only would His life and death be a substitute for my life, saving me completely, I would gradually be transformed into a person who would act like Jesus in every situation. I wanted God to change me into something better than I was. I was sick of "This is who I am, and I don't think I can change."

Unfortunately, I didn't understand what biblical transformation was. I didn't understand that the fruit of biblical transformation is a life that exhibits more joy, more mercy, more patience, more self-control, and more love for the people around me. Instead, I fell into a dangerous trap. I fell into a kind of pseudo-transformation.

One of the things I learned coming into Adventism is that we are to "come out and be separate," that our spiritual commitment should somehow make us different than people "in the world." But instead of going down the road of biblical transformation, I tumbled into the inevitable trap religious people sometimes fall into. Instead of changing from the inside out, in order to feel that I had changed and become "different," I settled for external ways to mark that I was different from those who didn't believe as I did. If I couldn't be transformed, then I was going to be doctrinally informed.

Adventism, because of its unique history and slant on things, carries with it this temptation. When a person makes all the right noises, and wears and eats all the right things, when they go to the church on the right day and serve on the right committees—all these things can become a substitute for biblical life transformation. In other words, some of us conclude that if we can't be genuinely holy, shouldn't we at least be strange? Some people allow outward appearances to be a substitute for inward transformation.

But to paraphrase the apostle Paul recorded in 1 Corinthians 13: "If I do all kinds of wonderful things in the name of my religion, even if I surrender my body to the flames for the cause, but don't have love, I gain nothing." Again, biblical transformation changes us from the inside out, and it is marked by greater and greater amounts of love, joy, peace, patience, kindness, generosity, faithfulness, gentleness, and self-control.

So, how does it work? Assuming that I'm interested in biblical transformation happening in my life, how do I go about it?

John Ortberg in his book *The Life You've Always Wanted,* explains how a life becomes transformed into a Christlike life by drawing a comparison between two ideas: trying and training.

Let's say you were invited by the Carnegie Institute to perform Rachmaninoff's Prelude in C-sharp minor at Carnegie Hall in one year. Your audience would be filled with dignitaries and heads of state, and you would be representing the best that the United States had to offer.

For months all you could do was think about that grand moment when you would walk out on that stage and play.

Finally the day comes. You are dressed in your rented tux with the long tails that maestros always wear. The applause is thunderous as you walk toward the 12-foot grand piano. You sit down, lay your hands on the keys, and suddenly remember—you don't know how to play the piano.

So what if, at that point, you decided to try, really, really hard to play Rachmaninoff's Prelude in C-sharp minor. What would happen? I mean you try harder than you've ever tried before. What would happen? I think at that point you would have to walk over to the microphone and utter the words, "This is who I am, and I don't think I can change."

I would venture to say that baptizing a person and then asking them to immediately try really hard to walk, act, and think like Jesus does is just as ridiculous as asking a person who doesn't play the piano to try really hard to play Rachmaninoff's Prelude in C-sharp minor.

Being transformed into a Christlike character is not a matter of trying real hard. In fact, there is nothing more frustrating than trying to overcome sin and be just like Jesus. No, it's not a matter of trying; it's a matter of training. Look at another verse from Scripture:

"Do you not know that in a race the runners all compete, but only one receives the prize? Run in such a way that you may win it. Athletes exercise self-control in all things; they do it to receive a perishable wreath, but we an imperishable one. So I do not run aimlessly, nor do I box as though beating the air; but I punish my body and enslave it, so that after proclaiming to others I myself should not be disqualified" (1 Corinthians 9:24-27, NRSV).

Paul is speaking of training here. He's talking about growing pains. He's talking about the whole process of sanctification. He's talking about transformation. Trying really hard to do something you're not prepared for is a sure path to failure. Training for something that is an ultimate goal is a sure road to growth.

Training to act like Jesus would act is the best way to avoid spiritual atrophy.

You know what atrophy is, right? When I was in college I blew a knee out playing basketball and had to have it in a cast for three months. When they took the cast off I couldn't believe how weak and skinny my leg was from nonuse. Not exercising my knee made it withered and weak.

The same thing will happen to those who don't exercise their spiritual life. It can wither and weaken to the point where they just aren't interested in spiritual things anymore. A person that doesn't tap into a life of spiritual transformation is a person who is stuck with *This is who I am, and I don't think I can change.* Read about it in the parable of the talents in Matthew 25.

It's the poor fellow who doesn't work with the talents given him that ends up outside of the will of the master. But conversely, the two men who worked with the talents that they were given were rewarded and given more.

Exercising our spiritual gifts, using God's power to actually do the kinds of things He'd like us to do on this earth, is the only way to transform into the likeness of Christ. It won't happen by accident. It's an invitation that we have to respond to with purpose.

The problem we face as a church is *What does real transformation look like?*

We'll look at that in our next chapter.

CHAPTER 9

ACTING CHOSEN—WHERE THE RUBBER MEETS THE ROAD

Overlooking the Obvious

Not too long ago I observed a funny thing at the student center of the academy where I am Bible teacher and chaplain. I was playing pool with one of the students when another student came over and asked if I'd seen where he'd put his key. As he stood there, sincerely asking me this question, I looked down and saw the key on a chain hanging around his neck. When I pointed that out, he gave me a sheepish look and silently walked out.

It was funny, but I couldn't laugh too hard. I can't tell you how many times I've spent good minutes looking for something, only to look down and see that whatever I was looking for was in my hand.

Sometimes it's easy to overlook the obvious. I once spent more than a half hour trying to fix our vacuum cleaner, only to find that it didn't work because I'd failed to plug it in. Even in our spiritual lives it's easy to overlook the obvious, especially considering what we know about being chosen by God. Sometimes we act as if being chosen means being members of an exclusive club.

Lessons From a Little Crook

Rumor has it that Zacchaeus was a wee little man, a wee little man was he. And he was a weasel, too. He would have cheated his mother out of her last nickel if it meant that he could continue his life of luxury and ease. You see, Zacchaeus loved the finer things in life—his home, his clothing, his car. I mean his horse. The point is, everything he owned was the best. But more than anything else, Zacchaeus craved attention. He loved hobnobbing with the higher-ups in society. He loved attending functions at the governor's mansion and being assigned one of the best seats of honor at parties. The problem was nobody liked him enough to invite him to any parties. It wasn't that he had developed any socially unacceptable, nasty little habits. It wasn't even that he wouldn't be any fun. Nobody in Jericho would invite him anywhere because most of them hated his guts.

And they hated him for a pretty good reason. Zacchaeus was Jericho's chief tax collector, the overseer of a lot of other tax collectors. And tax collectors tended to be a pretty dishonest bunch of people. It was their job to extort extra money from ordinary citizens with the threat of violence or imprisonment. If someone didn't pay what Zacchaeus demanded—even if it was twice the tax they really owed—he'd merely call the Roman guard and have them put in prison for not rendering to Caesar that which was Caesar's.

Zacchaeus was filthy rich, but socially and spiritually he was as poor as you can get. The only people who dared associate with him were those under his immediate control.

Then one day Zacchaeus heard that Jesus was coming to town. He left his mansion that morning with the high expectation that he was going to meet a very important man. As he rounded the corner and approached the center of town, he saw a crowd clustered around Jesus, who was walking down Main Street. Zacchaeus made his way to the edge of the throng and tried to squeeze in. In a heartbeat the people surrounding Jesus saw what was happening, and a very tall wall began to form, blocking the little man's way. Christ's disciples quickly caught wind of who was trying to get close to the Teacher and made sure that their guard was up too. After all, it wouldn't be good for someone like Zacchaeus to get too close. What would people think if Jesus were to hang out with the likes of Zacchaeus?

It didn't take long for Zacchaeus to be painfully aware that he wasn't welcome, but he wouldn't give up. He had to at least see

Jesus. He'd never seen such a fuss made over anyone before. That's when Zacchaeus resorted to the ridiculous. He saw the direction that Jesus was walking and knew that down the street, just over a block or so, was a sycamore tree. Running quickly ahead of the crowd, Zacchaeus climbed the tree. *Maybe if I get high enough and hide behind some branches, nobody will see what I'm doing,* he thought.

Imagine his embarrassment when Jesus stopped directly underneath the tree, looked up, and said, "Zacchaeus, come down. I'm going to your house today."

Neither the throng nor Jesus' disciples had any idea what was going on. What was Jesus thinking? Matthew, the former tax collector, may have leaned over and said, "Hey, Jesus, do You know who You're talking to here?"

But Jesus knew exactly whom He was talking to. And He and His disciples went to the little man's home and ate at his table, rested, and visited until late in the day.

It's funny what we do with that story. For some reason, when we tell it to our children we miss the big picture. Usually the moral lesson we take from this story is that Zacchaeus was so impressed with Jesus that he repented and paid money back to all the people he'd robbed, up to four times what he had taken.

Now that's a fine moral, and it's true. But if we stop there, or even if we make that the focus of the story, we're missing something very important that Jesus was trying to teach both His disciples and us today.

Let's notice that just before this all happened with Zacchaeus Jesus tells the disciples a story of two rich men (Luke 18). One was respected by the community, and one was not. He calls them a Pharisee and a publican. In the story, much to the disciples' discomfort, He makes the publican (or the tax collector) out to look good and the Pharisee evil. What kind of backwards thinking was that?

As He's teaching, some children come running up to Him. But the disciples try to block their way so that Jesus won't be bothered by the insignificant. After all, a child could never be important enough or influential enough to gain an audience with Jesus. Jesus paused in what He was doing, looked at His disciples, and said, "Hey, stop that! Let these children come to Me. The kingdom of heaven is made up of people like this."

If that didn't confuse the disciples enough, Jesus was approached by a rich man who asked Him what it took to get to heaven. Again, Jesus' answer makes everybody uncomfortable. He says, "First, keep the commandments." Notice the specific commandments that Jesus chose to mention, for they all relate to how we treat each other. Jesus knows human nature. And then He told the rich man, "Now, take care of all the poor people in your life; then come and follow Me." After some uncomfortable silence the wealthy young ruler crept away with his head down. And the disciples were even more confused.

Then as they neared Jericho a blind man started making a lot of noise trying to get Jesus' attention. Quickly the embarrassed disciples tried to quiet the man so he wouldn't bother the Master. But Jesus heard the blind man calling, so He stopped and healed him, sending him away with 20/20 vision.

Next came Zacchaeus. Do you see a pattern developing here? Jesus was trying to teach His friends a very valuable lesson. *Maybe the most valuable lesson.* He was trying to show His friends what it looked like to be a follower of God. He was trying to show them what should have been obvious all along to those who follow God.

Cut to the Chase

The disciples and the rest of the people who hung around Jesus treated others depending on how society viewed them. In other words, their motto was "Love your friends and important people, but it's OK to ignore or treat with contempt the insignificant, especially if you don't like them."

Jesus knew that nothing could be further from the truth. In fact, Jesus spent the bulk of His ministry trying to get it through the thick skulls of His disciples that the one identifying characteristic of His followers—of His chosen (or remnant, if you prefer)—is the overwhelming and unyielding love they show for the human beings around them.

Like He said to the rich young ruler, keeping the commandments and following the doctrinal truth that you're convicted of is important. It's very important. But if your doctrine is devoid of the actions of love, as our friend Paul the apostle would say, you might as well walk around smashing a couple of cymbals together. In other words, *a church with great doctrine and straight truth is necessary, but without love, it is just noisy and irritating to the people that they come in contact with.*

Truth Minus Love Equals Darkness

Just recently I heard a fellow faculty member tell a story that emphasizes the point Jesus was trying to make with His disciples. A sister of this faculty member had made some poor choices in life and found herself pregnant out of wedlock. When the scandal hit the church, one dear church member decided to throw a shower for the young mother and child. After the little baby boy was born, she sent out the invitations. The day came for the shower. The room was decorated, refreshments had been prepared. But nobody from the church showed up.

You can imagine the pain and embarrassment this young woman felt as she sat there waiting for her shower to begin. That pain carried over to the weekend, and she decided that it would be more comfortable for her if she were to stay home from church. So, wanting the little one to attend the children's Sabbath school, our faculty member—this unwed mother's sister—took her little nephew to church.

She walked up the steps and into the church. A greeter smiled at her, gave her a bulletin, looked down at the baby, and said, "Oh, is this your sister's little bastard?"

My friend turned around, left the church, and drove home. It was years before her sister darkened the door of a church again.

I think it's a good guess that the greeter may have read her Sabbath school lesson that week. She was probably a pretty faithful church member. She probably believed the right things about the Sabbath, the sanctuary, and the second coming of Christ. It's possible that she was a champion of the health message. But something was missing. Somehow, in her walk with the Lord, she was missing the obvious. She couldn't see the big picture.

Again and again Jesus and the New Testament writers emphasized the fact that if we can't treat each other well, then we have no place with Him.

In one of the most famous sermons ever delivered, the Sermon on the Mount, Jesus said, "It's easy to love your friends, but if you want to truly follow God's will for your life, if you want to call yourself chosen, then love your enemies" (see Matt. 5:43, 44). When a rich lawyer asked Jesus what it took to be saved, Jesus didn't answer him with a litany of doctrine. He told him the story of the good Samaritan (Luke 10).

When the disciples wanted to know what should distinguish them as followers of Christ above the rest of the world, Jesus could have said anything. He could have said, "You should dress a certain way, or believe these special things." But He didn't. He said, "People will know that you are My followers by how much you love each other" (see John 13:35).

The Bible says that God's chosen ought to be a peculiar people. The world should look at us and see that we live good, moral, clean, healthy lives. They ought to be able to see that we believe in the kind of peculiar doctrines that say incredible things about God and set us apart from other religions. That's all part of being chosen. But, if the world doesn't see that the most peculiar thing about us is the uncompromising, passionate way we love each other *and them,* all we are is a bunch of clanging cymbals with peculiar beliefs (see 1 Corinthians 13.)

Again and again the biblical authors were moved by the Holy

Spirit to write about the importance of loving each other and treating each other with godly love and respect. Just look at the evidence in Scripture. Besides Jesus' example, Paul writes in Philippians 2 that "we ought to regard others as better than ourselves" (see verse 3).

First John 2 tells us, "Whoever says, 'I am in the light,' while hating a brother or sister, is still in the darkness. Whoever loves a brother or sister lives in the light, and in such a person there is no cause for stumbling" (verses 9, 10, NRSV).

In 1 Peter 1, Peter writes, "Now that you have purified your souls by your obedience to the truth so that you have genuine mutual love, love one another deeply from the heart" (verse 22, NRSV).

Obedience to the truth, according to Peter, is loving one another with a mutual love, deeply and from the heart. We are not to just be polite to one another, or put up with one another. We are to love one another deeply from the heart.

Jesus Himself thought this truth was so important, He even went so far as to suggest that people who didn't have this kind of love would not inherit the kingdom of heaven. Read about it in Matthew 25. In the parable of the sheep and goats, the only criteria by which people are saved or lost is how they treated the people around them.

As you read the Bible, it's as obvious as the nose on my face (and that's pretty obvious). The key to living in God's will is to love one another. And as obvious as that is, somehow, like the student looking for his key as it hangs around his neck, sometimes we miss the importance of it all.

I hope I don't sound presumptuous when I say that this truth is as vital to Seventh-day Adventism as the doctrines of the Sabbath, the condition of humans in death, or the sanctuary doctrine. And the reason I believe this is, to quote a pastor friend of mine, "Nobody was ever brought to Jesus by somebody they didn't like."

But, sadly, another statement is just as true. Many people have been driven away from Jesus by Christians who didn't like them, or who treated them poorly.

Just as I was writing this chapter, I was told of a Seventh-day Adventist pastor who refused a single mother a dedication service for her baby because it was born out of wedlock. Can you imagine Jesus blessing all the little children except those who came from single-parent homes? What kind of thinking is that?

It's time we get our priorities straight. We learn the bad stuff when we are little, when we establish a pecking order in school. Remember the little kids who were picked on because they weren't good at sports or because they were chubby or didn't look quite right? We carry this stuff through our teen years into adulthood. We treat people as though they have to measure up to our standard of looks, behavior, or spirituality. And it's absolutely satanic.

Do you want to act like Satan? Then do his job and devour the saints. Be unkind (unloving), for any reason, to one of God's children. According to the Bible, that's as satanic as it gets.

It's time for God's chosen—you and I—to get it right. It's time to see the obvious. In these last days of earth's history it's crucial to follow the example of Christ, to love one another as He has loved us. When we allow Christ to so influence us, not only will we be a remnant church, we will become *remnant people.* Remember, churches don't lead people to Christ; people—led by God's Spirit—lead people to Christ.

Yes, being chosen is a privilege. *But being chosen despite what you and I know about ourselves is nothing more than grace to the nth degree.* You didn't do anything to be chosen. God chose you because He loves you.

And being chosen carries with it responsibilities. Our first responsibility is to develop the kind of character that loves those around us. Realizing we are chosen is the first step toward true godliness. Living as if we are chosen is the next.

The problem is, acting like one of God's chosen isn't something we can force. It has to come from the heart. It can't be faked, at least not for long. God's chosen are to go through a continual experience that will transform them into the image of Christ. This happens as we participate in the spiritual disciplines of prayer, meditation, spending time in Scripture and other inspirational literature, and practice unselfish service to others. Practicing these spiritual disciplines draws us closer into communion with Christ and implants His character in us.

Confusing Knowledge With Transformation

The problem with acting like God's chosen is that our churches are full of people who, for one reason or another, have not been transformed into the image of Christ. We want to be "peculiar," but for some reason we don't want to risk being transformed. So instead of spending time in spiritual disciplines, we find other ways to become peculiar, or, if you prefer, to act chosen.

John Ortberg, in his book *The Life You've Always Wanted,* puts it like this:

"We know that as Christians we are called to 'come out and be separate,' that our faith and spiritual commitment should make us different somehow. But if we are not marked by greater and greater amounts of love and joy, we will inevitably look for substitute ways of distinguishing ourselves from those who are not Christians. This deep pattern is almost inescapable for religious people: If we do not become changed from the inside out . . . we will be tempted to find external methods to satisfy our need to feel that we're different from those outside the faith. If we cannot be transformed, we will settle for being informed or conformed."

The temptation to let unique doctrine be the proof of being chosen is all too real in Seventh-day Adventism. Unique doctrine is a gift. It is an effective description of God's character. It plays a large part in what this church has been called to do on this earth. But if we allow unique doctrine to be what we're known for, we have completely missed out on the big picture. My hope is that we will become remnant people; people who can't help treating those around us with love and tenderness. I pray, personally, that I will become truly peculiar in the eyes of the world, just as Jesus was.

As we've seen in this chapter, being chosen carries with it the mandate to love one another. The Bible gives us even more details of what God expects from His chosen people. In the next chapter we'll break down the steps of God's calling for our lives in what I call God's "big three." This is God's bottom line for His chosen people. It's what being chosen looks like.

CHAPTER 10

BOTTOM-LINE GUY —CHOSEN TO ACT

Bottom-line Guy

Have you ever met someone who can't tell a story because they never get to the point? I know a guy who'll take 30 minutes to tell a 30-second story. I find myself getting irritated and saying, "Get to the point!" He usually pauses, remembers where he left off, and then keeps on talking. It's when I talk with this friend that I realize I'm a bottom-line kind of a guy. Don't beat around the bush with me, just cut to the chase, tell me what you want, and then I'll tell you whether I want to buy into it or not. It saves so much time.

I was still in high school when I realized that being a bottom-line kind of guy was a good way to go. A friend of mine was trying to set me up on a blind date with a friend of hers. When I asked what the prospective looked like, she said, "Oh, she's real sweet."

That made me want to know more. "Good, but what's she look like?"

Again, my question was avoided. "She's got a great personality!"

I never did get to meet this girl, but I'm guessing that she may have been (what's the politically correct term?) facially challenged. Just cut to the chase. Go bottom line with me and we'll both be safe.

It didn't take my wife long to find out that I'm a bottom-line kind of guy. As you know from earlier in this book, we were married five months after we met. Cut to the chase, get things out in the open, and everyone can move on with life, right?

About two months after we were married, Wendy and I were

driving home from a party where we'd enjoyed a good time with some friends. As we rode along I looked over at her and saw that she was crying. This was a new thing for me.

Guys aren't very good at dealing with women who cry. We don't know what to do. I pretended not to notice, hoping her tears would go away on their own. I turned up the radio. My mind was going a thousand miles per hour. Was her seat belt too tight? No, that couldn't be it. Did I do something bad? Maybe, but I couldn't remember what it was. I was at a total loss.

Finally we pulled into the driveway, and I had to shut off the car and acknowledge that the woman I had pledged my life to had a leaking face. I turned to her with the sensitivity of a man who is truly in touch with his feminine side and asked, "Uh, why are you crying?"

"I'm fine; don't worry about it." Why can't girls just say in plain terms what's bothering them? Most guys aren't particularly intuitive. We pretty much need pictures drawn with crayons in order to figure out what's going on.

"If you're fine, then why are you crying?" I asked.

She looked at me and said, "I don't know."

It took me three hours and a lot of amateur psychology to finally find out what the problem was. Unfortunately, the problem was me. I had done something to hurt my wife's feelings about two weeks before, and she had held it in to the point of finally bursting out into tears. When she told me about it, the incident was so far removed from my present train of thought that I had a hard time feeling bad about it. It was kind of like spanking your dog for wetting on the carpet two weeks ago. It has no idea what's gotten into its owner.

I apologized, and then asked my wife a pretty direct question. "Do you think we should get a divorce?"

The shock value of the question was enough to make her face start leaking again. I explained that if we were to stay happily married, we would have to have a different set of rules for communicating hurt and disappointment to each other.

That night we drew up a contract that we've abided by ever since. The contract said that we would give each other the courtesy of privately communicating hurt or disappointment when it happened, not two weeks after it happened. At that point the offender would apologize to the offended and promise not to do it again. Now, if you ever see my wife talking to me privately in the corner of a party, you know what's happening.

But it works. At least it has for us. Bottom line. If you need to tell me I'm an idiot, tell me. I can do something about it only if I'm aware of it. Cut to the chase with me, and life will be a lot easier for everyone involved.

God's Bottom Line

What about God? Have you ever wondered what God's bottom line for His chosen people is? Have you ever said, "If I decide to give my life to You, God, what's Your bottom line for me? What hoops do You want me to jump through, what do I have to give up, how am I supposed to act? Let's cut to the chase, God. What's Your bottom line for me?"

Throughout history people have answered this question in a multiplicity of ways. People have given large sums of money to churches and charities thinking that maybe this was what God wanted from them. Others have climbed up cement staircases on their knees in order to impress God with their determination. Still others go door to door trying to convince people that their religion is the truth and that there is no other way. People through the centuries have tried pretty hard to do the will of God in their lives, just to make sure, when push came to shove, that they were on His good side.

We even have people in the Seventh-day Adventist Church who try somehow to win God's favor. They're sure that His bottom line has something to do with finding the straight testimony (nobody has ever been able to show me where that is) and enforcing it on those not fortunate enough to know the truth as well as they do. I've always considered that kind of behavior as saying, "If you don't sin the way I do, then you can't play in my church." Being chosen has nothing to do with acquired knowledge or behavior. Nobody is chosen by God because of how well they adhere to truth. God chooses us because He created us, loves us, and wants to live with us for eternity. Period.

The search for what God expects from His chosen has taken many dips and turns, so let me clear something up at the start. The terms for salvation, according to the Bible, have never changed. If you want to spend eternity with God, if you want everlasting life, walk with Him. The Bible says it like this: "Believe on the Lord Jesus Christ, and you will be saved" (Acts 16:31, NRSV). In other words, live in Christ, follow the Lamb wherever He goes (Revelation 14:4), know Him, so that you will recognize His voice (John 10:27). This simple act has always been the biblical course to salvation. But, after you believe, after you have accepted salvation, after you have entered into the knowledge of being "chosen," what then? What's God's bottom line for you then?

I asked myself this question and thought about it long and hard. I read a lot of books, too, but I finally stumbled across a Bible verse that told me exactly what God wants from His chosen people. It's found in the Old Testament book of Micah. "This is what the Lord requires of you: to do justice, love mercy and walk humbly with your God" (see Micah 6:8). That's it. That's God's bottom line. This is what God expects from people who follow Him: to do justice, love mercy, and walk humbly with their God.

Do Justice

What does it mean to "do justice"? Most people don't have a hard time with this. Most of us have an innate sense of fairness that comes out at a very early age. If any of you had siblings, you know what I'm talking about.

When I was little, my mom would buy my sister and me one

candy bar. She would take it out of the wrapping and then break it in half, handing one half to my sister and one half to me. You know what happened? I yelled, "Her's is bigger than mine!"

"No, Mark's has more chocolate than mine." We'd sit there and argue about it until Mom would take the candy out of our hands and eat it herself. I think it was a clever ploy to eat candy guilt-free. The point is, my sister and I had this strong sense of justice from an early age.

I happened to be sitting in a graduate school class the day and hour that the O. J. Simpson trial verdict was to be read. The professor was lecturing while 40 people with little transistor radios were pretending to take notes. One group in the back of the classroom even had a miniature television, watching and waiting for the verdict. When the jury came out and the verdict was to be read, the teacher turned off his overhead, saying, "If someone wants to turn up their radio, we can all hear the verdict." Now, the classroom was split ethnically down the middle—about 20 Caucasians and 20 African-Americans. At the verdict, the weirdest thing happened. Twenty White people went, "Oh, no!" And 20 Black people jumped up and down and cheered. Why? It was how each group perceived justice. Our built-in, God-given sense of justice was at the core of our elation or disappointment at the verdict.

Hollywood makes a mint off of our want for justice. It's human nature to love to see the good guy get his day and the bad guy get his doom. God loves justice too. He has promised that when it's all said and done, the good guys will have their day and the bad guys will get their doom.

But, until that day, God tells us that His chosen must "do justice." He is asking us to live out what He has placed in our psyche from the very beginning. To do justice means to treat people fairly—how they deserve to be treated.

When we do justice, we give people what they deserve. Good or bad, justice demands a verdict. Justice rewards good behavior and punishes bad behavior. And God wants us to appeal to that sense of justice when we deal with people as a society and as individuals on this earth. He wants us to applaud good and boo evil.

But more than that, doing justice means that we cannot judge a person because of the color of their skin, the church they do or don't attend, the clothes they wear, or whether they listen to Howard Stern or Rush Limbaugh. When we truly "do justice," we try to set aside our assumptions and first impressions, and strive to base our reactions on the *quality of a person's character,* regardless of who they appear to be. *Justice knows no prejudice.*

When God asks us to "do justice," He's asking us to treat every person, regardless of our prejudice, with the dignity and respect that they deserve as a chosen son or daughter of God.

Love Mercy

The second expectation that God asks of His people is to love mercy. If doing justice means treating people like they deserve to be treated, then loving mercy means that sometimes we should treat people in ways they don't deserve to be treated. I found a supreme example of loving mercy at an academy where I worked. One of the faculty members who didn't have a reputation for being lenient, much less merciful, walked out a door one evening and nearly stumbled over a couple who were embracing more vigorously than school rules allowed. When he asked them to stop embracing and head for their respective dorms, the young man flew off the handle. He screamed at the faculty member, using a number of colorful metaphors, some of which had to do with this particular faculty member's family background.

Well, the stage was set. At faculty meeting that evening the story was told, and everybody expected justice to be done. It was just a matter of deciding whether to kick the kid out or send him to a firing squad. Instead, something else happened.

In tears, the offended faculty member suggested that the young man be suspended for three days. And since the student was from Florida, he suggested that he spend the three-day suspension at his—the offended faculty member's—house. "Maybe if he stays with us, we can mend the relationship and come out of this thing as friends instead of enemies," he said.

The motion was passed, and the young man stayed with the faculty member for three days. A friendship was rekindled, and the past became the past.

Sometimes—not always—but sometimes, doing justice isn't what God requires of us. God says that He wants His people to love mercy: especially when mercy can be more redemptive than justice.

Aren't we glad that God loves mercy? The Bible says that while we were still sinners, enemies of God, Christ died for us (Romans 5:8). Ephesians tells us that "He chose us in him before the creation of the world" (Ephesians 1:4, NIV). He did all of this in His mercy, knowing that many of His chosen would reject Him in the end. The Bible teaches us that the wages of sin is death, but the gift of the mercy of God is eternal life.

All of God's people, at one time or another, have had to appeal to His mercy in order to maintain their relationship with Him. And He has extended us that mercy. Now He asks us to return the favor and, when appropriate, extend mercy to one another.

Walk Humbly With Your God

Thinking about what it means to walk with God, two realities hit me. The first was the whole concept of going for a walk. What are you asking when you ask someone if they want to go for a walk? Two different walks I've taken illustrate what I'm talking about.

My father has a history of volatile marital relationships, and his relationship with his second wife was no exception. One day while I was downstairs doing some laundry, I heard a fight break out upstairs. There was the usual yelling and slamming of doors, but this time I heard a big *crack* and then a *boom*. I ran upstairs and found my dad in the hallway holding his face in his hands, and in a blind rage. My stepmother had hit him in the eyes with both fists, eventually giving him the look of a raccoon. After she hit him, she pushed him through the nearby doorway and locked him out of his room. I'd never seen Dad so furious. As I was running down the hall, he raised up and kicked the door off its hinges and started into the bedroom. I grabbed him just as he was entering, carried him out to the living room, and tried to calm him down. Finally I said, "Dad, come on; *let's go for a walk* and cool down."

When I asked Dad to go for a walk with me, he knew I wasn't asking him to get out and get some exercise. He put on a jacket, and we walked for about two hours. At first he walked furiously. Gradually he slowed down until he walked casually. It was on that walk that I started to know my dad for the first time in my life. As we walked stuff came out that I never knew about him. The walk calmed him down and brought him to his senses. *He reentered his house a calmer man with a new perspective* on how to handle his problem.

Tuck this story under your lip and let me tell you about another walk I went on that came out of a different circumstance.

When my wife and I were just getting to know each other (after my initial declaration of marital intent) I took her on a surprise date to Victoria, British Columbia. We took the hour-and-a-half drive to Vancouver, sailed on a ferryboat to Vancouver Island and drove to Victoria. We ate dinner together, then went for a walk. It was a warm spring evening with a light mist in the air. The lights on the harbor were illuminated in the mist, and Wendy and I walked, hand in hand, just talking with each other. It was on that walk that we began to truly know each other. It was on that walk that I got my first kiss.

When you ask somebody to go for a walk with you, you're asking them to spend some time with you—to get away from whatever distractions are in your life and get a new perspective. Going for a walk is time spent sorting things out. Going for a walk is communicating without distraction.

When God says He wants His people to walk with Him, I think

that's one part of what He's talking about. He wants His children to spend regular time away from the distractions of this life in communication with Him—just getting to know each other. He knows that sometimes we get ourselves wound up in a knot and need to get away and sort things out. A walk with Him is the perfect solution to some of the binds we get ourselves into.

Jesus did that on a regular basis. The Bible recounts that sometimes He'd go off by himself to spend time in communion with His Father. God extends that same invitation to His chosen, to you and me; to walk with Him. Going for a walk is part of God's bottom line for His chosen.

The second thing that struck me about walking with God was the question If I were going to literally go for a walk with God, what kinds of things would we do as we walked together? I decided to look in the Gospels to learn what Jesus did while He walked on earth.

I discovered that what He did most was to attempt to make the lives of suffering people more livable. He went out of His way to pay special attention to the insignificant in society. And by doing so He exhibited God's character, making it visible to the people around Him.

I think that's the other dimension of walking with God, another part of His bottom line. God wants His chosen to walk this earth as His representatives. He wants us to walk this earth as if we were walking with Him, showing kindness and relieving suffering when presented with the opportunity to do so.

Walking with God is a part of God's bottom line because, ultimately, walking with Him creates in us the kind of character that makes a difference in this world.

Have you noticed that the ingredients to God's bottom line are remarkably similar to the Ten Commandments? It's not by accident. Loving God and loving your neighbor are the two main principles that make up the Decalogue. Micah 6:8 is just a cool twist on what God gave to humanity at Sinai a long time before.

You Have Heard It Said . . . (Taking the Minimum to the Maximum)

God's bottom line has been the same since the foundation of the world. In *Patriarchs and Prophets* Ellen White tells us that what God always wanted from His followers was that they obey His law. Doing justice, loving mercy, and walking with God are nothing more than God's law in different terms. Instead of giving us a list of minimums that we can't do, God, through the prophet Micah, gives us three positive things that we can do. He makes the law proactive.

As we read the Bible we can see that God has attempted to deepen the level of our understanding of what it means to obey Him. It seems that He had to start at square one with Israel. They needed to know what *not* to do. God started at first base with them, giving them the bare minimum that it would take for them to act like God's chosen. And He expected them to grow from there.

Think about it for a moment. The Ten Commandments are the minimum you could do for God and for your neighbor. The *least* you can do for God is remember Him one day a week. The *least* you could do for Him is to avoid bowing down to an idol. The *least* you can do for your neighbor is to not murder him, or steal from him. The Ten Commandments are the *minimum* that we can do for God and for our neighbor.

I believe that through the centuries God has called His chosen to new levels of understanding His law. The law hasn't changed, but hopefully our understanding of it has. As people in the Bible grew in grace, God attempted to take His law out of their hands and place it in their hearts (Jeremiah 31:33). While on earth, Jesus called His followers, His chosen, beyond the minimum. He didn't say, "I've come to give you the very minimum you need to survive." No! He said, "I've come to give you abundant [maximum] life" (see John 10:10).

God doesn't want His chosen to live life to the minimum, but to the maximum. That's why Jesus, in the Sermon on the Mount, called His followers to a higher standard. He took the minimum standard as the people understood it at Sinai and challenged His listeners to a higher understanding of the law.

"You have heard that it was said, Don't murder. I say to you, if you hate someone you are guilty of murder" (Matthew 5:21,22). Do you think the Israelites took the commandment to the same extreme at Sinai?

In the Sermon on the Mount Jesus said, "Loving your friends is easy. Everyone does that. I say to you, 'love your enemies' " (see verses 43, 44). That's a far cry from "an eye for an eye and a tooth for a tooth," a commandment given at Sinai to Israel (see Exodus 21:24).

Jesus called His chosen to go beyond the minimum. He challenges His chosen ones to go to the maximum in their obedience to Him. Again, not to earn salvation, but as a matter of devotion. He said, *"If you love Me,* keep My commandments" (John 14:15, NKJV). Don't keep them out of obligation, or out of fear. Keep them because you have embraced being God's chosen. He died and secured you a place in eternity. He extended grace to you when you were still in rebellion toward Him. Keep His commandments to the max because you can't help being madly in love with a God who would take such good care of His children.

Jesus said that all of the law and the prophets—*all of them*—hang on this: that His chosen ones love God and God's children like He has loved them (Matthew 22:37-40).

If, somehow, your obedience to God has held you back from loving contact with the people in your life, caused you to spiritually excommunicate any of God's children, or left you with no desire to save the lost, *then question your obedience,* or at least your understanding of God's law.

Avoiding evil is not the standard of obedience. Yes, avoiding evil keeps us out of trouble, but simply avoiding evil is not true obedience. God's law, rightly obeyed and understood, produces proactive compassionate love and understanding. When you have the law in your heart, you aren't just *avoiding* evil; you are *doing* good. God's law, rightly practiced, is justice, mercy, and a walk with the One who chose *you* before the creation of the world.

One of the reasons people don't act chosen is that they have a big misunderstanding of who God is. My experience has taught me that this comes from people's life experiences. In the next chapter we'll take a look at who God is, and who He isn't.

CHAPTER 11

WHAT YOU DON'T KNOW COULD HURT YOU

While I was attending the seminary, one of my professors told the following story.

It was at the height of Germany's domination of Europe during World War II that John, a middle-aged man, decided he wanted to make a difference. He had lost his wife to an illness, and his children were grown and taking care of themselves. So instead of sitting down and feeling sorry for himself, he decided to join a little-known resistance movement established to thwart the Nazis by hiding and protecting the Jews that lived in his city of Brussels, Belgium.

He knew that by so doing he would be risking his life, but he felt moved to do it. He'd heard about the underground anti-Nazi movement through a friend, and approached that friend to volunteer his services.

John's friend arranged for a meeting in an otherwise anonymous house in a neighborhood close to his. As they entered the study of the house, an older gentleman with an unwearied demeanor greeted John suspiciously. Introductions were made, and the older man sat down at a desk across from John.

"How can we help you?" asked the man.

"I want to help you. I've heard that you need people to help in efforts against the Nazis. I'm too old to fight, but I can do whatever you ask."

After a long hour of interrogation the older gentleman seemed to be satisfied that he could trust John. His final admonition was this: "If you join our effort against the Nazis, you must give me your word that you will abide by two rules. You must do whatever we ask, exactly as we ask you to do it. You must never question the judgment or integrity of what we are asking. Do not ask 'Why?' Just do what we ask. Can we have your full cooperation in these two areas?"

John vigorously nodded in agreement.

"Fine, then. Be here tomorrow morning at 10:30, and don't be late."

The next morning John walked into the house right on time. Again he was met by the older gentleman. "Do you know the city?"

John knew the city like the back of his hand. He nodded.

"I need you to take this bag of groceries to the big blue house on the corner of Third and Fifty-second streets. You will find a garbage can on the west side of the house. Put the bag of groceries into the can, put the lid on the can, and then walk home any way you want. Do you know the house?"

"Yes, I know where it is," responded John. "Are we feeding a Jewish family in hiding?"

"Ask no questions! Do you remember the rules? I need you here every morning at 10:30 to do this for me. Can you do this for us every day, without asking questions?"

"Yes, of course," John stammered. "I'm sorry. I'm just glad to be helping in any way I can. You can count on me every day."

The man handed John the groceries and a map highlighting the streets he was to go down to get to his destination. But the directions were crazy. Yes, they got him to his destination, but in a crazy zigzag roundabout way. He knew a way to the house that would take him less than half the time, but decided not to question the man's motives, lest he get his head bit off again. Maybe the long way around was to confuse any attempt by the enemy to follow him.

He left the house and followed the exact directions given him and found the big blue house. He put the groceries in the garbage can, placed the lid on the can, and walked home. It made him feel good to know that he was helping feed a starving Jewish family.

The next day John showed up again, on time. He was handed another bag of groceries and the same map. Again he followed the map to the house. When he lifted the lid off the garbage can, the groceries he had placed there the day before were gone. He replaced them with the new bag, secured the lid, and walked home.

For weeks John did as he was told, feeling good about the fact that he was probably helping some family in hiding live through the terror of Nazi occupation.

And then one day something was different. He walked the same route with the groceries, but found that the bag he had placed in the can the day before was still there. Was something wrong? Had something happened to the family that was receiving the food? Should he ignore the order to ask no questions and tell his contact person that the family wasn't getting their food anymore?

He decided to just keep his mouth shut and do what he was told. After all, maybe the family couldn't get to the food on that particular day. Maybe tomorrow both bags of food would be gone.

But the next day John found that neither of the bags had been touched. Day after day John placed bags of food into the can until he couldn't fit any more in. The food that was in the can started to mold, and the new food was left out by the side of the can for the dogs and cats of the neighborhood to get to. It was becoming quite a waste.

It was all John could do not to ask a question . . . something . . . anything. Did his contact person know what he was doing? Each day he gave John a map and a bag. Did he know that his food was going to waste? A family two houses down from where John lived had six children. He knew they barely had enough to eat. They were probably hungry enough to eat the food that was being eaten by the rodents by the side of the garbage can next to the big blue house.

Finally, one day John worked up the nerve to ask his contact about the mission. "Sir, about the groceries I've been delivering . . . "

The man didn't even let him finish his statement. "No questions!" he shouted. He shoved the bag and the directions into John's hands and rushed him out the door.

John was frustrated. Once again, he started following the same out-of-the-way, crazy directions to the big blue house. As he walked he got angrier and angrier at the colossal waste of food that he witnessed every day. Wouldn't his neighbor and six children benefit from the food more than the rats in the alley next to the big blue house? Certainly they would.

He made up his mind two blocks into his journey. Surely if his contact would have listened and known that all that food was going to waste, he would have found a hungry family somewhere else. Obviously the Nazis had gotten to the family he was supposed to feed.

So, about three blocks into his journey, he turned around, walked home, and gave the bag of groceries to a very hungry, very grateful family in his neighborhood.

That evening nearly 1,000 Jews died or were captured by the Nazis in Brussels because of John's decision.

What John didn't know was that he was the signal for them to stay in hiding. Each day, between 10:30 and 1:00, they were to look for John carrying a bag of groceries by their hiding places. If they didn't see him walk his route, it meant that the coast was clear and that it was safe for them to come out from their hiding places.

The Salvation of Obeying

As Seventh-day Adventists, we have an interesting slant on obedience, don't we? It's a crucial part of our theology. We actually tie it into our theology of salvation. Now, don't get me wrong; we don't teach that obedience is what gets you into heaven. No, salvation is by grace, and grace alone. But we do tie obedience into our theology of salvation—let me explain.

Seventh-day Adventists don't teach that salvation is a *point-in-*

time event that happens in a person's life. Other denominations have a different understanding, teaching that you are saved at a certain point in time.

One time while I was with a youth group in downtown Seattle, a drunk street person walked up to me and asked what I was doing. I told him that I was with a local church group handing out sack lunches to people who were hungry.

He asked, "Are you Christians?"

I said, "Yes, we're from the Seventh-day Adventist church."

He said, "I'm a Christian! I was saved one day back in 1972 when I was baptized at one of the mission houses! Praise the Lord!"

A lot of people point to a certain place or time and say, "That's when I got saved."

Seventh-day Adventists believe and teach that salvation isn't a point in time, but a continuous process.

I didn't get saved; I am being saved! It's not something that happened, it's something that is happening. It's a process.

Yes, there was a point in time when the whole process began—a baptism, or an altar call. But the process didn't stop there. According to the Bible, that was just the beginning of a process that we call salvation.

As a review, the first part of the process of salvation is called *justification*. That occurs when, out of conviction of sin, you come to Christ for the first time and confess your sins, repent of them, and accept Jesus as your Savior. When we do this, we receive justification. In other words, because of Christ's death on the cross for us, God looks at us as though we had no sin on our record. Even though we may be guilty, He looks at us as though we had never sinned. That's justification.

And justification isn't a onetime event in our life either. How many times have we been convicted of sin in our lives since then, and have had to confess and repent all over again?

Even so, we believe, and the Bible teaches (Romans 8:1) that once we go through this first stage of the salvation process, in Christ, there is no condemnation for us. At that point we are being saved. But is that all there is to salvation? Is the justification of our sins the end of the process of salvation?

No. There's another stage of salvation, the second of three. It's sometimes referred to as *sanctification*. If justification is the starting point of salvation, sanctification is the evidence that there was a starting point at all. If justification is what happens when we come to Jesus, sanctification is what happens to us as we continue to walk with Jesus. If justification is acknowledging our being chosen, sanctification is learning to act like we've been chosen.

In a nutshell, sanctification is what happens when God's Spirit works in us to produce the fruit of obedience. In Romans 1 Paul calls it the *"obedience that comes from faith"* (verse 5, NIV).

We do it with our kids' all the time, right? We bring them through a human process of sanctification. We don't just ignore our kids' behavior after they are born. No; if we did, we'd have a bunch of social deviants running around the country. (OK, maybe some people did ignore their kids after they were born.)

We don't ignore our children's behavior. Because of the love relationship we desire to have with them, we mold it from when they are little. We teach them to obey. We do this for a variety of reasons, don't we?

First, we teach them the basics, the elementary rules of obedience so that they won't hurt themselves. We teach them not to touch the stove because it will burn them. We teach them to look both ways before crossing the street and not to play with matches. Our kids don't know it at the time, but all of these rules have their safety and their happiness in mind. They might really want to touch the stove, but we ask them not to. We know that if they obey, they will be happier and safer in the end.

But we don't just stop teaching them obedience at the elementary level. We move beyond obedience simply for safety's sake to teach them how to get along with each other. Share your toys; don't kick girls; help little old ladies across the street. We want them to get along well as social beings in society. We want them to do well in life, and to achieve that one must learn to obey certain social laws.

But we don't stop there either, do we? Not if we are good parents.

What's the ultimate goal of teaching your kids obedience? What are we after?

We hope that the obedience our kids learn will develop in them the kind of character that—when they reach adulthood—will produce a lifestyle that will make us proud of them. Ultimately, we hope that their cultivated character will produce a deep and lasting bond of love between us and them. And we hope their lives will reflect well on who we are, don't we?

Have you ever seen that before? Moms and Dads bragging about their kids? But even more than that, have you ever seen the kind of parent-child relationship that is thicker than any mere friendship? It's a combination of godly respect, friendship, and love that produces true agape between adult parent and child. It's a wonderful thing to behold.

In the spiritual realm, that's what God's goal is for us in the part of salvation that we call obedience or sanctification. Learning how to obey is just a step-by-step process in becoming inseparable with our heavenly Father.

Much like in a parent-child relationship, God starts us the same way He did the children of Israel, with some pretty basic rules. Some of the first rules we learn in our spiritual lives are the Ten Commandments.

As I've mentioned in another chapter, when looked at in the light of simple obedience the Ten Commandments are the base minimum one can do in order to be called a child of God. And for some of us, just keeping the Ten Commandments is challenge enough. But God wants to bring us beyond this kind of elementary obedience, to broaden our understanding of what it means to really obey Him. He doesn't want the just bare minimums from us. He wants the maximum. He didn't come to give us an OK life. He came to give us life abundant.

That's why Jesus took what we find in the Ten Commandments and broadened the whole scope of what it means to obey Him in the Sermon on the Mount. He said such things as: "You have heard that it was said to those of ancient times, 'You shall not murder'; and 'whoever murders shall be liable to judgment.' But I say to you that if you are angry with a brother or sister, you will be liable to judgment; and if you insult a brother or sister, you will be liable to the council; and if you say, 'You fool,' you will be liable to the hell of fire (Matthew 5:21, 22, NRSV).

Well, that's a little different than "Thou shalt not kill," isn't it?

Again, Christ takes another of the Ten Commandments and does the same thing to it.

"You have heard that it was said, 'You shall not commit adultery.' But I say to you that everyone who looks at a woman with lust has already committed adultery with her in his heart. If your right eye causes you to sin, tear it out and throw it away; it is better for you to lose one of your members than for your whole body to be thrown into hell" (verses 5:27-29, NRSV).

What is Jesus saying here in the Sermon on the Mount, and for that matter during His whole life on earth? He's doing what Hebrews 8 calls *taking the law out of our hands, and putting it in our hearts.*

He goes beyond the minimum and asks of us the maximum in obedience. It's not just enough for us not to kill or steal from each other anymore. No, we are to love our enemies. Instead of just tolerating another, this new kind of obedience asks us to drop what we are doing, seek out the one that we have offended, and make things right before we go on our way.

The new level of obedience that Jesus wants to develop in His followers moves us from the minimum of merely not harming one another into a life of proactive love for one another.

When He came to earth Jesus brought obeying God to a whole

new level. In a sense, He really raised the standard. He told us that He's looking for a new creation in His followers. That's a pretty big challenge isn't it? Wouldn't we all like to live a life that produces the kind of obedience that comes from the heart—the kind that would find us treating the people around us as God would have us treat them? I know I'd like that for me.

But guess what? Ultimately, God doesn't even want to stop there with you. Did you know that there's another type of obedience, an even higher level in the process of sanctification that God desires to mold into your character? There is.

It's called the obedience of intimacy. Yes, God wants you to know and obey the Ten Commandments. And yes, beyond the 10, He wants you to know and emulate Jesus' life and teachings about how we ought to treat one another. For some of us, stopping at that kind of sanctification will be the work of a lifetime. But His ultimate goal for us in obedience goes a step beyond that.

This kind of obedience—the obedience of intimacy—comes from a deep, sustained relationship with a loving, personal Savior. It's the kind of obedience that, over time, Abraham developed with God. The kind of obedience that has its ear so in tune with God's Spirit that when God asked Abraham to take his only son, sacrifice him, and burn him on an altar, Abraham didn't question where the voice telling him to do this strange, terrible thing was coming from.

Revelation 14 describes the people who acquire this kind of obedience as those who "follow the Lamb wherever he goes" (verse 4, NIV). These are people who can truly be described as "loving the Lord their God with all of their heart, all of their soul, all of their mind, and all of their strength."

Can you claim that? Can I claim that? Have I for even one full day loved the Lord with all of my heart, all of my soul, all of my mind, and all of my strength? I wish.

It's the kind of obedience that would find a person more willing to die than to offend God by sinning against Him, or by sinning against one of His children.

It's the kind of obedience that produces a finely tuned ear to the Spirit of God. It's the kind of relationship with God that puts all of the clutter and noise of this life in the back seat, so that the Spirit can nudge us to respond to His call to act when He beckons us.

You know what I'm talking about, that gentle nudge that you've felt from the Spirit. "Go speak to this person" . . . "Call that person and encourage them" . . . "Tell this or that person how you feel about your faith" . . . "Go and make things right with your son or your daughter."

It's the kind of obedience that daily responds to God's callings. It's the obedience Jesus had because of His intimate relationship with His Father. It's the kind of obedience that I want so badly to be a part of my everyday life.

God's desire is to produce in our lives this kind of obedience, not so much to make us better candidates for heaven, but to make us useful on earth.

Again, none of these stages of obedience are requirements for salvation, but they are all a part of the process of salvation—a part of being chosen. You become saved, and are being saved when you come to Christ. The Bible says, "Believe on the Lord Jesus Christ, and you will be saved" (Acts 16:31, NKJV). But you go through the process of sanctification (learning how to obey) as a result of walking with Christ.

Hebrews 10:14 puts it this way: "For by one offering He has perfected forever *those who are being sanctified*" (NKJV).

We could never obey well enough to get ourselves to heaven. If you want evidence of that, just look at your track record. Obedience is an outgrowth of a relationship with a God who wants to produce in you the kind of character that will show the world what He is like.

And ultimately, don't we all want an abundance of the fruit of the Spirit in our lives? Wouldn't we all love to experience an abundance of love, joy, self-control, patience, kindness, and generosity? Wouldn't we love to have that kind of obedience? I know that I would.

Spending intentional time walking and communicating with God is the only way to develop *that* kind of obedience, that which comes from the heart. The only way we can truly keep His commandments is by loving Him. And the only way to love Him is to get to know Him.

But it takes a willing heart. It takes a heart that desires to do its best, to give its all to honor God. Is that something that you want?

If it is, God will grow in you, and you will become more like Him. You will learn to obey. I know it doesn't seem like it sometimes, but it *will* happen. And if you are frustrated with your obedience track record, remember, He's in charge of that part of your life. He will be faithful to work this out in you. Just remember to put yourself in a place where God can speak to you on some sort of a regular basis. Spend some time in His Word; spend time talking with Him about your life.

And soon you will be able to shout with joy on that day when we will all experience that final phase of our salvation. That's the day we get to see our Savior face to face. That's the day that we will hear the joyful words from Jesus, "Well done, My good and faithful servant."

CHAPTER 12

"ANGRY AT GOD—SOMETIMES I DON'T FEEL VERY CHOSEN"

Through my life I've discovered that there are two kinds of anger. The first kind explodes in short, vicious flare-ups when something unexpected ignites the fuse of someone with a temper. From time to time, when I was a child, my dad demonstrated this kind of anger toward me. Some of the worst of it came during the times he'd try to quit smoking. I learned this the hard way.

When I was about 7 years old, my dad, unbeknownst to me, decided to kick the habit. Now, this happened during the summer when I was home all day, giving me the opportunity to be even more annoying than on a typical school day. This particular week I'd been in trouble with my father for both doing what I shouldn't do, and not doing what I should. Feeling as though I was on his bad side, I thought I'd try to make up by playing a trick on him. I decided that when he came in from work this particular night, I would hide behind the door, jump out, and scare him.

It was his fifth day without a cigarette, and I'm sure his body was screaming for nicotine as he unsuspectingly entered the house. I jumped out from behind the door and screamed, "Rawwwww!"

I don't quite know what happened next. My mom and sister tell me that I ended up in the living room behind the couch. They say I made it there *without* walking. When I came to my senses, my dad informed me that I would be going to bed without any supper that night.

Years have passed. As I'm writing this, I've just spent part of my Christmas vacation with my father. He told me that of all the regrets he has now, losing his temper and cuffing me over the head was at the top of his list. I told him that it was OK. Hitting me on the head didn't leave any lasting damage. But I appreciate his apology.

That's an example of one kind of anger. The kind of anger that flares up, strikes, and then goes away. Most of us have either dealt with it or felt it at one time or another. Maybe it's the kind of anger James and John, the "sons of thunder," exhibited on occasion.

Another Kind of Anger

Another kind of anger, one common to many of us, is brought on by an event or series of events that have left a person feeling disillusioned and bitter. And that bitterness eats away at their soul until it manifests itself in their very character. Unless it is dealt with, this anger produces the kind of bitterness that estranges friends and loved ones. It ultimately points the finger of blame *at God Himself.*

I've felt that kind of anger. I don't think I'll ever forget it. I was 19 years old, working in a fast-food restaurant in Seattle, when I received a phone call. A voice on the other end told me that my mother had been rushed to the hospital, apparently in a coma.

When I finally reached the hospital, tests had been completed. My mother had a tumor the size of a tangerine on the top front part of her brain. They were going to operate. The doctor sat down and told me that Mom would probably be a little different after the operation. It was even possible that her personality would change dramatically.

I remember walking into the room where my mother lay, now out of surgery. Her clean-shaven head was bandaged. Her eyes were black and blue and nearly swollen shut. As I took her hand, she looked up at me and asked, "Who are you?"

That hurt. You see, my mom was the kind of mother who would die for her children. Countless times she opened her home to teenagers who'd been in trouble or kicked out of their house, helping them until they could get back on their feet.

As she lay there in that hospital bed, a church member came in and tried to explain to me that God worked in mysterious ways. I didn't have much to do with God back then, but when I heard that God may have had a hand in what happened to my mother, I got a bitter, angry feeling about Him. I went away blaming Him for what happened to my mom, a woman who had done nothing but act like Jesus for as long as I had known her. The least He could have done was prevent the tumor from happening in the first place.

I was experiencing the kind of angry feelings that seem to be a part every person's human experience. Being angry at and blaming God when we are touched by evil seems to be synonymous with being human.

Let me further illustrate.

Years ago I was the chaplain of an Adventist college. Among many other duties, I had volunteered to coach the women's volleyball team. My requirements for making the team were three: you had to be a good volleyball player, you had to have at least a C average in your schoolwork, and you needed to participate in the spiritual life of the team.

The team became kind of a small group that shared its everyday concerns and prayed together. As the season went on, I noticed through various on- and off-court activities that one of my players had only two out of the three qualifications going for her. She was an excellent volleyball player and an exceptional student. But when it came to participating in the spiritual life of the team, she was silently and bitterly cold. When she did speak up, she was obviously antagonistic toward spiritual things.

When I called her into my office to ask her why she wasn't interested in spiritual things, I was met with cold stares and silence. I probed a little, and finally she broke down. Through convulsive sobs she revealed that from the time she was 3 until she was 12 years old her father had raped her. And often, later on the same day, he'd stand up in their church pulpit and preach about family values and love. Now 19, she was still waiting for him to acknowledge that he had wronged her, had destroyed her innocence. Even to say simply, "I'm sorry," or "I love you." She ended her confession with a final blow.

"I'm so angry," she said.

"Whom are you angry at?" I asked.

"I'm angry at God," she said. "What kind of God would sit there and let a young girl be raped by her father? He just sat up there, wherever He is, and let it happen. He didn't want to have anything to do with me then, so I don't want anything to do with Him now."

In time this young woman communicated to me that she believed strongly in God, but that she was sure He had found something in her life that warranted the terror that she had endured as a child. She was sure that God had some sort of sinister dark side that would show itself when He was displeased with the way she acted.

The cause of this young woman's anger is obvious. But was her anger misdirected? Was my anger misdirected? Is it OK to direct one's anger toward God, blaming Him for the evil things that fall into our lives?

Is That You, God?

Accusing God of doing evil is nothing new. The Bible includes the story of a guy named Job who had a pretty bad streak of evil happen to him. All his children were killed in a tornado. He lost all of his assets, including his savings account. To make matters worse, he came down with a terrible skin condition that left him with large oozing boils from head to toe. His anguish was mental, physical, and spiritual. These tragedies, this personal loss, shook Job to the foundation of his soul. Whom did he blame? Read the book of Job, specifically chapters 8 through 10. Here are some excerpts from these chapters.

"That is why I say, 'He [God] destroys both the blameless and the wicked.' When a scourge brings sudden death, he mocks the despair of the innocent" (Job 9:22, 23, NIV). "If only there were someone . . . to remove God's rod from me, so that his terror would frighten me no more" (verses 33, 34, NIV) "I loathe my very life; therefore I will give free rein to my complaint and speak out in the bitterness of my soul. I will say to God: Do not condemn me, but tell me what charges you have against me. Does it please you to oppress me, to spurn the work of your hands, while you smile on the schemes of the wicked?" (Job 10:1-3, NIV). Your hands shaped me and made me. Will you now turn and destroy me?" (Verse 8, NIV).

It's kind of obvious how Job felt, isn't it? Job, like many others through earth's history, placed full blame for the evil that tried to destroy his life on God. And many times, like Job, we become angry at God because we think He is putting us through disaster after disaster—not unlike the feelings of my young volleyball player friend.

How does God respond to these accusations?

He sent His Son, Jesus, to come and live with us. *Jesus came to earth to reveal the Father, to clear up our misconceptions about God and show us who He is and what He is like.* Without a doubt, when Jesus lived on earth people believed that it was God who brought evil into their lives. They thought that anyone who suffered a terrible misfortune or a debilitating disease was the victim of an angry God—a God with a dark, sinister, masochistic side.

Jesus Tried to Set the Record Straight

It wasn't long before Jesus had an opportunity to clear up this misconception of God's character. In John 9 we find Jesus walking along with His friends. There, on the side of the road, they see a blind man begging for money. It was widely known that this man had been born blind.

"Who sinned, that this man was born blind?" the disciples asked. They accepted the common assumption that God brought this terrible misfortune into the man's life as a punishment for some sin that he, his parents, or his grandparents committed.

"'Neither this man nor his parents sinned,' said Jesus, 'but this happened so that the work of God might be displayed in his life'" (verse 3, NIV).

In other words, Jesus says *God didn't blind this poor man, but since it has happened, let's use the situation to show how much more powerful God is than the evil that comes into our lives.*

He'll Take the Blame

Jesus came to reveal to us that God is not the author of evil and that He does not bring evil into our lives. In fact, the Bible teaches us just the opposite. James, the brother of Jesus, wrote: "Don't be deceived, my dear brothers. *Every good and perfect gift is from above,* coming down from the Father of the heavenly lights, who does not change like the shifting shadows" (James 1:16, 17, NIV).

First John 1:5 says that "God is light; in him there is *no darkness* at all" (NIV).

So who is it that brings evil upon the people of this world? Who is the author of the hideous things that happen in our lives?

The Bible describes an evil, spiritual being that exists in the world today. We call him Satan. The Bible describes him as a roaring lion, stalking and seeking those whom he can destroy. The Bible says that he is the cause of sickness, pain, destruction, and confusion. And he loves it when we blame God for the disaster that strikes our lives.

So What's a "Chosen" to Do?

So what do you do when you're mad at God?

The first step is to recognize that God is not the author of pain and evil. Instead, God is the provider of good things and wants to use bad circumstances to increase our faith and show that good is always more powerful than evil and that love is stronger than hate.

Second, when we are mad at God, the worst thing we can do is give Him the silent treatment. Again and again the Bible tells us of people so angry at God or their situation that they shake their fists at

Him, even yelling at Him. Read the Psalms or Job or Judges to find just a few examples of this. In each case God intervenes, settling the issue to the satisfaction of everyone involved. God can work with mad people.

However, if you turn your back on God, He will not force Himself into your situation. God created you and me with free wills to make choices to do good or evil; to communicate with Him or to ignore Him. God will never force Himself into a life that doesn't want Him there. If you're angry at God, yell at Him, scream at Him, tell Him how you feel, but please, whatever you choose to do, don't ignore Him. It's when we ignore God that we take ourselves out of His comforting hands and place ourselves in the hands of the spiritual power of this world, the true author of the pain in our lives.

The simple fact is we live in enemy territory. The Bible says that the prince of this world, the power of darkness, is active in bringing pain and discouragement to all he can. It doesn't take more than one half hour news broadcast to convince us anew that this is true.

And as innocent as God may be in the whole scheme of the evil and the sin that taints our lives, in a very large sense He chooses to take the blame. When Jesus laid His life down on the cross, He bore the brunt of all the evil, all the cruelty that anyone on earth could ever experience. When He laid his life down on the cross, He accepted the blame for all sin. Second Corinthians 5:21 tells us that "for our sake he made him to be sin who knew no sin, so that in him we might become the righteousness of God" (RSV).

All of the pain, all of the injustice, and all of the sin in this world were placed upon Jesus as He died that dark day on a cross.

Whatever you are feeling about God, remember that Jesus felt what you feel, encountered what you encounter, and is now inviting you to experience the healing that a relationship with Him can provide.

And finally, in the midst of your suffering, and in the midst of your anger, there remains a promise for you, God's chosen. Jesus said that He would not leave you in this world to suffer unto death. He said He would come back and make all things new. He promised that He would provide for the people who love Him—His chosen—a new heaven and a new earth, where all of the old things have passed away.

Near the end of the book of Revelation we read:

"And I heard a loud voice from the throne saying, 'Now the dwelling of God is with men, and he will live with them. They will be his people, and God himself will be with them and be their God. He will wipe every tear from their eyes. There will be no more death or mourning or crying or pain, for the old order of things has passed away'" (Revelation 21:3, 4, NIV).

I'm looking forward to that day. No more birth defects. No more brain tumors. No more abusive fathers. God's chosen will be home at last.

No matter what evil has happened in your life, you *can* trust God.

Get to know God for who He really is. Are you angry with God? He'll take the blame. Do you want to be healed of it? Then go to Him, talk with Him. Open your heart to Him and experience the healing and the hope that only He can give.

And if you've spent most of your life "unchosen," living apart from God, you may hesitate to go to a loving God with your messy past. Letting your past become a roadblock to your growth in Christ is a common hindrance to living a rich life in Christ. If this is the case for you or somebody you know, I've got good news. Read on.

CHAPTER 13

HOW CHOSEN IS CHOSEN?

God's Mulligan

I think every golfer has a mulligan story. This is mine.

I remember my first attempt at the game of golf. It was an interesting experience. I was around 17, and my dad took me to a beautiful golf course right outside of Seattle. It had a beautiful view of both Mount Rainier and the Cascade Mountains. I'd been looking forward to this and had done all that I could to prepare. I'd gone to a driving range a few times. I'd watched a golf video with my dad. I had even gone as far as to actually watch golf on TV (that's sort of like watching grass grow).

Dad and I drove into the golf course parking lot, and we were met by two of his friends. All of them had golfed for years. Me, I didn't know what clubs to use for each shot, and I knew nothing about golf course etiquette. All I knew was: Grab the club like a baseball bat and swing as hard as you can. I didn't have golf clubs of my own, so my dad let me use his.

One of my dad's friends teed up first. He lined up his shot and smacked that little white ball right down the middle of the fairway. His partner lined up and did just about the same. Then my dad lined up. He wound up and clubbed the ball 230 yards down the fairway, landing his ball just about where he wanted.

Then it was my turn. Dad handed me his driver, and I placed my ball on the tee, just as the men before me had done. I grabbed the driver like a baseball bat, lined up, and swung with all my might. I heard the ball *CRACK!* as I connected. It felt good. There was only one problem. The fairway was straight ahead of me. Very sharply to my right was the parking lot we'd just come from. My ball sailed into the parking lot at about 120 miles an hour. Dad and his two friends yelled "Fore!"

We lost sight of the ball, but we heard a loud noise. It sounded like what you'd hear if you dropped a 50-gallon fish tank off of a 10-story building. We dropped our clubs and ran to the parking lot. There we found a pickup truck with some new and unusual body work. There was a big crack in the passenger-side window, and the side mirror lay in shattered pieces just beneath the passenger side door.

A man ran out from the clubhouse and identified himself as the owner of the truck. We exchanged addresses and phone numbers, and returned to the first tee. I was pretty embarrassed and quite shaken up by the whole ordeal. But it wasn't the truck I was concerned with. It was my golf score. I didn't want to start my first golf experience in the hole. I looked at my dad's friend who had the scorecard in his hand, and asked, "So how many strokes does that cost me?"

He looked at me and said one of the neatest things I've ever heard. He said, "Don't worry about it. Just take a mulligan." I had no idea what he was talking about. I thought maybe a "mulligan" was another club that would better connect with the ball or something. He went on to explain that a mulligan is a do-over. You get to swing again and it doesn't count against your score. It's as if you were swinging for the very first time.

What a concept. I was so happy. I teed up again, wound up, and struck the ball. It dribbled about 10 feet in front of me, then stopped. I was just glad that I didn't break anything else.

I Need a Do-over!

As a kid, I played all kinds of games with my friends. Whether it was four square, kickball, or some other game, we had an uncomplicated rule. If you didn't like the way you did something, you'd just call "Do over!" With those two words your mistake didn't count in the final outcome of the game.

I can't tell you how many times in my life I've wished that I could stop after a stupid mistake, look back at the thing I messed up or the people I'd hurt, and shout, "Do over! I'll take a mulligan!"

During my first year as a boys' dean we had a kid named Jack at the school. You could describe Jack as a little more than hyperactive. One evening I called the guys to worship and Jack came in looking like he'd just mainlined a pound of sugar. This kid was bouncing off the walls. All of the other guys came in and sat down, but Jack continued to bounce around like his feet were on fire.

Calmly I said, "Jack, sit down, it's time for worship." He didn't pay any attention. Again I said, "Jack, sit down; it's time for worship." Again he ignored me. Finally I said in a loud, stern voice with a hint of irritation, "Jack, sit down now!"

Jack turned, frolicked right over to where I was sitting, and started dancing and singing, "You can't make me, you can't make me, nanny nanny boo boo, you can't make me!"

As he stretched his left arm toward me, I grabbed it, placed my other hand in the middle of his chest, lifted him up, and placed his back (not very gently) on the floor. I put my foot on his chest and pulled and twisted his arm to further get his attention.

As I pulled up on his arm I heard a loud *pop. That* prompted me to let go, and Jack ran up the stairs to his room in tears. I had my assistant dean cover worship, and ran upstairs after him. I found Jack curled up on his bed, sobbing.

I asked if his arm was OK. He said it was. "So why are you crying?" I asked.

Jack proceeded to tell me about how he was being treated at home—by his parents. The stories he told me, which I later checked and confirmed, explained this poor kid's behavior. His bad behavior had always been corrected with violence, and once again, I confirmed in his mind that using violence to solve undesirable behavior was acceptable. Even in a safe Christian environment.

I needed a mulligan. I just wanted to shout, "DO OVER!" I wanted to be able to rewind the videotape of my life and just do everything different. But I couldn't. What was done was done. There was no way of telling what kind of consequences my sin was going to have in the life of this young boy.

Why can't life be more like golf? Why can't we just take a mulligan when we need it? Everyone needs a mulligan every once in a while.

I've got good news for you. In a very real sense, chosen people are provided with mulligan after mulligan, whenever they need them.

First John 1:9 tells us that if we confess our sins to God, He will provide us with that mulligan. Forgiveness is ours for the asking. Chosen people are forgiven people. A terrible price was paid for our sins. Because Jesus took the blame and the penalty for our sins—no matter what they are—we have forgiveness as His chosen (Colossians 3:12-13; Ephesians 1:3-7). I'm thankful every day to serve a God like that.

But there's always the question "I know that works for the little stuff, but what about the really big stuff? You know, the stuff that I don't just fall into. The stuff I do on purpose."

Good question. Does God dole out mulligans for habitual sin, the sins we do on purpose?

But What About the Really Big Stuff?

Once when I was teaching an adult Sabbath school lesson in my local church, I asked a question that got a pretty strange response. "Does God forgive sins that a Christian does on purpose?" I asked.

Nobody answered. They just looked confused.

"Let's say you're faced with a situation—a temptation—that gives you a chance to think about it for a while. You know that it's wrong to do whatever it is you're tempted by, but after thinking about it a while, you go ahead and do it anyway."

By now confused looks turned into horrified ones. I asked again, "Is God willing to forgive sins that are committed like that? Sins that are committed with premeditation?"

Slowly heads began to shake in a negative direction. Finally an elderly woman sitting in the back raised her hand and said, "No, there's no room in God's kingdom for people who act like that. If God forgave sins like that, then there'd be no incentive for people to resist temptation."

Another way to pose this question is to ask, "How chosen is chosen?" If you're walking with God, the Bible calls you His chosen. How easy is it to get unchosen? Is it simply a matter of doing something wrong on purpose? Let's look at one of many Bible stories that should give us all a new appreciation for God's grace toward chosen people.

Killer Lust

It was springtime, the time of year when kings send their armies out to battle. At least that's how 2 Samuel 11 records it. On this particular evening, King David was trying to sleep, but couldn't. I don't know if it was too hot or if he was worried about a particular battle that his commander in chief, Joab, was fighting, but David was restless.

After tossing and turning, David decided to climb the stairs to his rooftop and sort out his thoughts. As he stepped up there, the view took him by surprise. Looking down, he saw a beautiful woman standing in a tub of water, taking a sponge bath. There was a full moon, so the view was pretty good. He turned away. He knew that it was wrong to dwell on lustful thoughts. But he turned back. He just couldn't keep his gaze from her. After a while she finished her bath and went back into her home.

David went back to bed and tried to sleep, but this time his mind was not on war. The thoughts dancing through his mind were thoughts of lust and impurity. Thinking and fantasizing about her wasn't enough. He had to have her. And David was the king. He could have what he wanted.

He called a servant and told him to summon Bathsheba for a private meeting in his bedroom. Bathsheba was escorted into the king's chambers, David asked the attendant to leave, and he committed adultery. I know that we like to romanticize what happened. We like to make Bathsheba a willing partner, but let's not do what Hollywood does to Bible stories. David was the king, and she was his subject. He knew she was married. Her husband was a soldier in his army. Despite that, David wanted her, and he wanted her *now*. A woman in that day and culture had no say in the matter.

The Bible says that when David had finished with her, her sent her back home.

A few weeks later David got a letter from Bathsheba. The letter's message: "I'm pregnant." David's whole life flashed before his eyes. He weighed his options, and then came up with a plan.

He sent to the battlefield for Bathsheba's husband, Uriah. Uriah was just a private in the army, so he couldn't figure out why the king would want to speak with him. When he got to the palace he was brought to the royal office, where David began to chitchat about the war. Finally Uriah asked respectfully, "Why did you want to talk with me?"

David came right out with it. "I want you to go home and spend the night with your wife." Uriah left the palace, and David thought his plan had worked. If Uriah slept with his wife, her pregnancy could be easily explained.

The next day David's men reported to him that Uriah hadn't gone home. Instead, he slept in the barracks with some other soldiers. David couldn't believe the nerve or the devotion of Uriah. He called him back to the palace. "I thought I told you to go home last night."

"O, king, I cannot go home and sleep with my wife while my fellow soldiers are suffering out in the battlefield."

David couldn't believe his ears. He went to plan B. He invited Uriah for dinner that night. Uriah, still not understanding why he was getting all this attention, honored the king's request and joined him that evening for a meal fit for a king. But David wasn't interested in feeding Uriah. The Bible says that David got Uriah drunk. Surely, if David were to send a drunk soldier out to his wife, he would make it home and spend the night with her.

Not a chance. Uriah was a man of honor. Even drunk, he had enough reasoning not to think of himself when his fellow soldiers were in the thick of battle. That's when the king proceeded to plan C.

You know the story. David told his commander to charge the city they were fighting, then withdraw suddenly, leaving Uriah on the front line—an unsuspecting sitting duck. Joab did as he was told, and Uriah died an innocent man, faithful to his king.

Bathsheba was allowed to mourn the allowed time, then was taken by the king as his newest bride. David must have looked like a good person to those in his kingdom. After all, he was taking in the widow of one of his faithful soldiers, who now had no means of support. David was just glad that he got away with premeditated adultery and murder. *And David would have gotten away with murder and adultery if he hadn't been one of God's chosen.*

You see, God treats His chosen ones better than that. Even when we premeditate hideous sin, and commit those sins on purpose, God goes to extremes to not let His chosen die in their sin. God sent the prophet Nathan to confront David. When David knew that he was busted, he did some serious repenting. Would David have ever confessed if it wasn't for Nathan? Probably not. Who knows?

The fact is, after Nathan finished with him, David needed a mulligan. And he took one. Look at what he wrote to God as a response to his guilt. It's found in Psalm 51:

"Have mercy on me, O God, according to your steadfast love; according to your abundant mercy blot out my transgressions. Wash me thoroughly from my iniquity, and cleanse me from my sin. . . . Purge me with hyssop, and I shall be clean; wash me, and I shall be whiter than snow. Let me hear joy and gladness; let the bones that you have crushed rejoice. Hide your face from my sins, and blot out all my iniquities. Create in me a clean heart, O God, and put a new and right spirit within me. Do not cast me away from your presence, and do not take your holy spirit from me. Restore to me the joy of your salvation, and sustain in me a willing spirit. Then I will teach transgressors your ways, and sinners will return to you. . . . O Lord, open my lips, and my mouth will declare your praise. For you have no delight in sacrifice; if I were to give a burnt offering, you would not be pleased. The sacrifice acceptable to God is a broken spirit; a broken and contrite heart, O God, you will not despise" (verses 1-17, NRSV).

Can God forgive intentional sin? Even if we have to get caught red-handed before we admit our wrong? Did God forgive David? Hebrews 11 shows us that He did. Let's not forget who we are dealing with here. God loves His chosen so much that He will do anything He can to reclaim and redeem them.

Read Luke 15 to see the extent that God will go in order to bring his sheep/coins/lost sons back into the fold. Was the prodigal son acting in rebellion when he took his inheritance and spent it on drugs, sex, and rock and roll? Of course he was. When he came slinking back home, what was his father's response? Was there a lecture waiting for him? Was there even a hesitation on his dad's part in receiving his son back in the family?

Nope. None whatsoever. In fact, the son walked away with the family ring, the best robe in the house, and a fatted calf.

If you are a God follower, it's important for you to know that God considers you His chosen one. You are safe with Him. He's not going to hold you out of heaven on some sort of technicality. You are being held by the mighty grip of God. To get out of that grip will require the kind of effort that can only be described as total and sustained rebellion against the One who has chosen you.

God's Tight Grip

Before we examine further your assurance of salvation, I'd like for you to read some of what the Bible has to say about the subject. Please take the time to read these texts carefully.

"For no one can lay any foundation other than the one that has been laid; that foundation is Jesus Christ. Now if anyone builds on the foundation with gold, silver, precious stones, wood, hay, straw—the work of each builder will become visible, for the Day will disclose it, because it will be revealed with fire, and the fire will test what sort of work each has done. If what has been built on the foundation survives, the builder will receive a reward. If the work is burned up, the builder will suffer loss; *the builder will be saved,* but only as through fire" (1 Corinthians 3:11-15, NRSV).

"My sheep hear my voice. I know them, and they follow me. I give them eternal life, and they will never perish. *No one will snatch them out of my hand.* What my Father has given me is greater than all else, and *no one can snatch it out of the Father's hand"* (John 10:27-29, NRSV).

"And this is the testimony: God gave us eternal life, and this life is in his Son. Whoever has the Son has life; whoever does not have the Son of God does not have life. I write these things to you who believe in the name of the Son of God, so that *you may know that you have eternal life.* And this is the boldness we have in him, that if we ask anything according to his will, he hears us" (1 John 5:11-14, NRSV).

"Keep your lives free from the love of money, and be content with what you have; for he has said, *'I will never leave you or forsake you' "* (Hebrews 13:5, NRSV).

"All that the Father gives me will come to me; and him who comes to me I will not cast out" (John 6:37, RSV).

After reading these texts, I hope you can concede that—at the least—it is very difficult, almost unheard-of, for a chosen person to slip out of the grace-filled grip of God's salvation.

But can it happen? Yes, the Bible says it can. In passages such as

Hebrews 6:4-6 and Galatians 5:4, the Bible does teach that falling out of grace can happen. We just need to look at the Old Testament story of King Saul to tell us that. But it seems to be a *strange act,* an *unusual happening.* You don't see it much in the Bible. In fact, you see just the opposite.

When we seriously consider many of the biblical characters we should see all kinds of people who just didn't make the cut. Instead, we see people like Samson, David, and Jephthah listed in Hebrews 11 as people of great faith.

Have you ever read the story of Samson? For most of his life he killed people and slept with prostitutes. Basically, even though he was chosen before birth for a special work for God, he turned his back on it. How is it that he will be in heaven? You can be sure of this: It's not because of anything he did.

You see, God never gave up on him. And at the very end, when Samson—blinded and bound—reached toward God with his heart, God heard his prayer. And Hebrews 11 tells us that he is counted as one of God's faithful.

Samson, David, Jephthah. and you and I are going to be saved, not because of our faithfulness to God, but because of God's faithfulness to us. We don't have anything to offer. The Bible says that the best we have to offer, the holiest stuff we have in us, is just a pile of filthy rags (Isaiah 64:6). No, we are assured of salvation because of what Jesus did, and not because of anything we have done.

And because of what Jesus did for His chosen, we can have complete confidence, complete assurance, that we are being saved. God's chosen are heavenbound. Jesus said that if we believe in Him, we *have* eternal life and because of that we don't even have to go through judgment (John 5:24).

I can't think of words filled with more assurance than that.

As Christians, as God's chosen, it's extremely important that we understand this. How can we have a convincing conversation with a person unaware of God's grace if we can't tell them *with assurance* what God has done for us? If we don't even know that God's grace is saving us, what kind of good news is the gospel? We would need to adjust John 3:16 to say, "For God so loved the world that He gave His one and only Son, that whoever believes in Him, *has a possibility* of not perishing, and *maybe* just *might* receive eternal life." I don't know about you, but if John 3:16 were to read like that, I'd find another religion.

Are chosen people perfect? Nope. But are they being saved? Thoroughly. Is there any reason whatsoever to doubt God's word about the security of His grip on us? I've not found one.

For chosen people, the cross is their mulligan. It's their do-over. Even for the big stuff. It's their hope, their future, and their security.

Final Thoughts

My sincere prayer? That this book has confirmed in you the knowledge that you are a chosen person, adopted by God as His son or daughter for no other reason than He loves you. I do pray that you will grow in God's love and find opportunities to share this good news with the people in your life that so desperately need to hear it.

My hope? That when you acknowledge your choosing, you will one day look back on your life and see that God was there beside you all along, guiding your path to fit into His plans for you.

My great desire? That we can all become the kind of people that can learn to love each other and live together in peace. That's what church is supposed to be. I'm still learning how to do that. My desire is that we can all become one with God as we become one with each other. Chosen.

What a feeling.

What a privilege.

What a responsibility.

Let's live our lives every day in a way that shows the world around us what being chosen is all about.

Mark—11 months old, 1962.

Mark's mother and father (Bob and Pat Witas) in 1957.

Mark with Mom, 1962.

Mark with Mom, 1964.

Mark with Grandma and Mom, 1964.

Mark and his family in 1968.

Mark and Wendy on their wedding day, August 4, 1985.

Mark baptizing cousin Sarah, 1998.

Mark with son Cole at 4 days old, 1997.

Mark and birth mother at the sand dunes in Oregon, 1991.

Mark at seminary graduation with (left to right) Louis and Jeanette (birth mom and her husband); Wendy and Aunt Marilyn; Grandma Judson in front, 1996.

Mark, his sister, Lori, and her son Taylor in 1996.

Birth aunt and family. From left to right: Grandma Carter; Uncle Lee; Aunt Marilyn (birth mom's sister); cousins Jacqueline, Sarah, and Elizabeth; and birth grandma Judson. Taken October 5, 1996, after Jacqueline's and Elizabeth's baptism.

Mark with Louis and Jeanette at Madison Academy graduation in 1998.

Mark and Wendy at Mark's ordination with Elder Ron Schmidt in 1998.

Grandpa Louis and Grandma Jeanette with Cole, my son, in 1998 at the Peace Arch Border Crossing—British Columbia/Washington line.

Mark's birth mother and her husband (Louis and Jeanette Bruner)

Don (Mom's husband), nephew Taylor, and Mom, 1995.

Mark with Jim and Pam Tait and Alex Bryan, a seminary friend, 1999.

Mom and Don in 1999.

Mark's dad (Bob) with Cole in 2000.

Mark and Wendy Witas in 1999.

Mark, Cole, and Wendy at Pacific Union College graduation in 2001.

Birth family at Mark's graduation at Pacific Union College in 2001.

Summer of 2001: Dad (Bob), sister (Lori), and Mark at the Biltmore Estates, North Carolina.

Dad (Bob), Mark, Cole, and Wendy in 2001 at the Biltmore Estates, North Carolina.